A SOLDIER'S PROMISE

LAURA SCOTT

READSCAPE PUBLISHING, LLC

A SOLDIER'S PROMISE

by

Laura Scott

A SOLDIER'S PROMISE

Book 2 in the Crystal Lake Series

Please Note

This is a work of fiction. Names, characters, places and incidents are either the product of the author's imagination or

CRYSTAL LAKE SERIES (LISTED IN ORDER)

*Stories with Linked Characters

"Hey, Jules—we have two trauma patients on the way, ETA less than five minutes."

ER nurse Julie Crain stifled a groan. She'd just returned from taking her previous patient down to the morgue, and she was emotionally drained from dealing with his grieving family. She forced her exhaustion aside. "Okay, what's the story?" she asked, glancing up at Merry Haines, the ER charge nurse at Hope County Hospital.

"A two-vehicle crash, T-bone on the driver side. From what I hear, the drunk driver who ran a red light and caused the crash wasn't hurt-but the guy in the SUV and his young daughter are being brought in."

Julie caught her breath as her heart thumped painfully in her chest. Oh, no. Not a young child. She couldn't handle an injured child. She closed her eyes and prayed.

Please God, keep the little girl safe. And her father, too.

"I hope they lock up the drunk driver and throw away the key," Merry muttered.

She understood where Merry was coming from.

Working in the ER, they'd both seen more than their fair share of alcohol- or drug-related injuries and deaths.

Dr. Gabe Allen came into the room in time to catch the last part of their conversation. "The driver was Tommy Hinkle," he said with a dark scowl. "So yeah, I think that scenario is highly likely."

Not a tourist then, but one of their own. Tommy Hinkle was the Crystal Lake troublemaker, picking up where his father had left off. At nineteen, he wasn't even legal to drink at all, much less drink and drive.

Tommy would end up in jail this time, for sure. Just like his father. The only good thing was that his mother, Annie Hinkle was still recovering in a Madison rehab center from a terrible car crash and wasn't here to see her son behind bars.

Before she could check over their supplies, the doors from the ambulance bay burst open, and a bevy of paramedics wheeled in two gurneys.

Julie was relieved to be in position to take the first patient, which happened to be the father.

"Thirty-year-old Derek Ryerson, suffered loss of consciousness at the scene," the paramedic announced. "We placed two eighteen-gauge PIV's and gave a liter of fluid so far. His vitals remained stable throughout transfer."

She quickly connected the heart monitor leads to his chest, reassured by the steady beat of his heart. She leaned over to perform a neurological assessment, noting an abrasion on the side of Derek Ryerson's left temple that was easily seen, considering his military-short dark hair. Concerned about a possible head injury, she carefully lifted his eyelids and peered at his pupils. She flashed her penlight, grateful to note they were both equal and reactive.

She continued her assessment, listening to his heart and his lungs. The right side of his lungs didn't sound as clear as his left side, and there was an angry red band across his chest from where the seatbelt had held him in place, likely preventing additional and more serious injuries. When she brushed a hand over the right side of his ribcage, he let out a low groan.

Bruised or broken ribs? Or something worse? She glanced up again at the heart monitor, but his vitals continued to be stable.

Before she could call over to Dr. Allen, a large hand reached out to grab her wrist. She gasped, her gaze clashing with his as he stared at her intently. His hard, blue, uncompromising gaze caused a spurt of fear.

"My daughter. Lexi," he said hoarsely. His pain-glazed eyes bored into hers, and his grip on her wrist tightened painfully. "Where's Lexi?"

The flash of fear faded when she realized he was concerned about his daughter. She glanced over to where Merry and Gabe were examining the young girl. "Don't worry. Lexi is right here in the gurney beside you. My name is Julie and I'm your nurse. Merry and Dr. Allen are taking good care of your daughter."

Lexi must have heard her father's voice, because up until now, the silent child created a sudden commotion from the gurney next door as she struggled to get away from where Merry was trying to hold her down. "Daddy! Let me up! I wanna see my daddy!"

"Lexi." Derek dropped Julie's wrist and struggled to push himself upright as if intending to go to his daughter. He didn't get far before he let out a harsh sound and grabbed the right side of his chest, swaying dangerously. His face went pale, beads of sweat popping out on his forehead.

"Take it easy. You're going to hurt yourself more," Julie told him, trying to keep calm, knowing she didn't have the strength to hold him down if he chose to get up. Derek Ryerson was a big man, at least six feet tall and broad shouldered—his entire body was solid muscle. Whatever he did for a living, he kept in shape. "You have a couple of bruised or broken ribs, and we haven't cleared your spine yet, either. We also need to make sure you don't have a head injury."

For a moment, he stared into her eyes, as if trying to decide whether or not to believe her. Considering the strength with which he'd grabbed her wrist, she thought he couldn't be too badly injured. She waited, simply looking back at him, secretly amazed at how brilliant his blue eyes were.

Good thing she was immune to good-looking men.

After what seemed like a long time, he dragged his gaze from hers. "Lexi, listen to what the doctors and nurses are telling you to do, okay, honey? They're only trying to help. I'm right here next to you. I promise I won't leave without you."

"Daddy, I want my daddy," the girl cried out between heartbreaking sobs, repeating herself over and over again, seemingly inconsolable. The poor child must be traumatized from the accident.

"Gabe? I might need a chest X-ray here," she called out, doing her best not to be distracted by Lexi's sobbing mantra, even though she wanted nothing more than to cross over to offer comfort.

Gabe walked to her side. "His vitals, along with his oxygen saturation, are stable, so let's do a CT scan of his head, neck, chest, and abdomen. That way we'll have the big picture."

"Sounds good." She picked up the phone and called over to radiology to put in the request for the CT scan. When she finished, she turned back to Derek. "How does your head feel?"

"Fine," he said through gritted teeth. The lines bracketing his mouth indicated suppressed pain, but whether from just his ribs or his head, too, she couldn't say for sure. He closed his eyes, as if he couldn't stand the bright lights. "I'm fine, just take care of my daughter."

She frowned. Was his head injury worse than she thought? Hadn't she already told him that his daughter was being cared for? "Merry and Dr. Allen are taking good care of Lexi, remember? Does your back hurt anywhere? I need you to be honest with me, because if you have a cracked spine that goes undiagnosed, you could become paralyzed."

He opened his eyes and glared at her, but she refused to back down. She couldn't understand why he was downplaying his injuries. "No, my back doesn't hurt. My neck is sore, and my head hurts a bit, too. The right side of my chest feels like it's on fire, but nothing hurts as much as listening to Lexi cry."

She smiled gently, feeling bad for him. She could only imagine how difficult it would be to stay on a gurney if her niece had been injured. "I know, and I'm sorry. But the best thing you can do for your daughter is to make sure you're all right. She needs you."

"I'm fine, nothing a little aspirin won't cure. Bruised and battered from the airbag and the crash, but fine."

There was no point in arguing. She glanced over at the next gurney, where Gabe and Merry where in deep conversation.

"I don't see any sign of serious injury," she heard Merry saying to Gabe. "The paramedics believe she was likely in a proper booster seat in the back on the passenger side, opposite from the point of impact. When they arrived, they found her out of the seat and clinging to her father. Apparently, they had a heck of a time getting her away from him, and they had to give her a mild dose of Versed to get her onto the gurney. She's probably fine, but we should get a chest and abdominal CT scan, just to be sure there is no internal bleeding from the straps of her car seat."

Julie waited until Merry finished. "Since they both need CT scans, I should take them down the hall to radiology together. I think Lexi will be calmer if she can be with her father."

"She can't go into the scanner with him," Gabe pointed out with a frown.

"No, but I could sit with her in the viewing room, behind the lead glass," she argued. "And once Lexi sees her father going through the scanner, maybe she'll cooperate when it's her turn."

Gabe and Merry looked at each other and shrugged. "Fine with me," Gabe finally agreed.

Satisfied, Julie waited for Gabe to finish his exam of Derek and then entered the necessary radiology orders for both patients into their respective charts.

She made the arrangements and then quietly told Derek the plan. "I'm going to put Lexi in a wheelchair and have her sit with me in the viewing room to watch you go through the scanner first. The machine makes some loud noises, which can be scary. I want to reassure her it doesn't hurt."

His expression was guarded. "Are you sure she's well enough to sit in a wheelchair?"

His protectiveness for his daughter made her smile. "Amazingly, Lexi doesn't seem to have any injuries at all," she assured him. "But we'd like to get a body scan just in case there's some internal bleeding. Kids aren't always good about being specific with their aches and pains. Or maybe she gets that streak of stubbornness from you."

For a moment, a flicker of grim amusement flashed in his eyes in response to her gentle teasing, and he subtly relaxed. "All right," he agreed. "If you think it will help. Can I talk to her while I'm in there?"

"Not while they're scanning. You'll need to stay still and hold your breath when they tell you to. You can talk to her before and after, though."

"Okay." He lifted his hand and gingerly rubbed the right side of his chest.

"Show me exactly where it hurts," she said, noticing the gesture.

The stubborn look came back into his eyes, and she feared he was going to deny any pain at all, but he gently fingered the area where his lowest ribs were. "Right here, mostly. You were probably right about the cracked ribs."

"Maybe. Or you could have some damage to the lower lobe of your lung or damage to your spleen." She figured blunt honesty was best, so he would understand the seriousness of his situation. "Your breath sounds were a bit diminished on the right side, but the CT scan will tell us everything we need to know."

He reached out to grasp her wrist again. "If they have to take me to surgery, I need you to promise you'll look after Lexi."

Stunned, she gaped at him. Look after Lexi? What on earth did he mean? "Is there someone I can call for you? Her mother? Grandparents? Friends?"

"There's no one to call," he said flatly. "Lexi and I are on our own."

She swallowed hard and nodded, desperate to reassure him. "All right, but try not to worry. I'm sure you'll be fine."

He didn't let it go. "Promise me. If something happens, I want you to look after her. Don't let strangers take her away. Promise!"

———————

DEREK KNEW he probably sounded like a lunatic, but he didn't care. The pain along the right side of his chest was bad, far worse than he'd let on, and after what the petite brunette nurse had said about the possible damage to his lung, he was very much afraid that, once they'd completed the scan, they'd whisk him off to surgery.

He'd downplayed his injuries because he didn't want to stay overnight in the hospital, unless, of course, Lexi needed to be observed. No matter what, he was not going to leave his daughter. Lexi had already been through so much, more than any six-year-old should have to handle. With her mother dead and buried, she needed him now, more than ever.

If only he'd stopped for something to eat earlier, he wouldn't have been driving through the intersection at the same moment as the idiot who'd run a red light, slamming into them.

"Daddy?"

He turned his head, hiding a wince, to look at his daughter. True to her word, the pretty nurse—what in the world was her name?—had gotten Lexi into a wheelchair and brought her over to the side of his gurney. He forced a broad, reassuring smile. "Hey Lexi, how are you feeling?"

Her solemn gaze didn't waver from his. "Fine," she whispered. "Can we leave now?"

If only they could. He'd been all set to leave without the scans until the nurse had mentioned the possibility of a cracked spine. At this point, he needed to know exactly what he was dealing with. Besides, he needed to be sure Lexi was all right, and if that meant getting a scan first, so his daughter could see it wouldn't hurt, then that's exactly what he'd do. He held his daughter's gaze, holding his smile in place. "Afraid not, baby-doll, first we have to get checked out by the kitty-cat machine." Lexi wasn't easily distracted, especially when she wanted something. But that didn't stop him from trying.

"I don't want to stay here." Lexi's eyes, blue like his, revealed a hint of fear. "It's scary."

The pretty nurse, he couldn't read her name on her ID badge because his vision was blurry, another tidbit he hadn't fessed up to, came over. "Lexi, we need to make sure your daddy's not seriously hurt. So we're going to take him for a CT scan, but you can watch from behind the glass the whole time, all right?"

Lexi barely spared the nurse a glance. He wanted to apologize for his daughter's behavior, but there was no point, since Lexi had no idea she was being rude.

"Okay, let's go," the woman said in a cheerful voice. She went behind Lexi's wheelchair to push her forward, while his gurney was maneuvered by a tall guy who was likely some sort of orderly. When the gurney went over a bump, he had to clench his teeth against a surge of pain. He focused on the nurse, who was talking to Lexi.

"We'll be finished with these scans in a half hour, Lexi," she was saying in that same cheery tone. "See the clock on the wall up there? It's seven o'clock in the evening. Do you know how to tell time?"

Derek was surprised when Lexi's head moved in a barely

discernible nod. His daughter was listening, even if she didn't appear to be paying attention.

"The big hand is on the twelve, and we'll be all finished before the big hand gets down to the six."

Lexi glanced at the clock but said nothing more. The lack of response didn't stop the nurse's rather one-sided conversation, and he was grateful she didn't pass judgment on his daughter the way so many others had.

The way Lexi's grandparents had.

The CT scan didn't take long, and as soon as they were finished looking into his head, he talked briefly to Lexi, reassuring her. Then he had to stay quiet until the rest of the scan was completed. When the scan was complete, he heard the nurse encouraging Lexi to take her turn.

His daughter, bless her stubborn heart, wasn't too keen on the idea. When he saw Lexi's wheelchair come closer, he turned his head toward her. "Lexi, we can't leave until I know you're safe and healthy. The kitty-cat machine doesn't hurt. All you have to do is to close your eyes and let them take pictures. Once I know you're fine, we'll leave."

He could see the instant flare of protest in the nurse's eyes at his rash promise, but he glared at her, silently threatening her not to contradict him. She pressed her lips together firmly but didn't say anything.

Lexi finally agreed to the scan, and he watched protectively as the nurse allowed his daughter to climb down from the wheelchair and up onto the CT table by herself. He had to give the woman points for being astute—she seemed to instinctively know that Lexi wouldn't tolerate being touched or carried by a stranger.

After the orderly came back to push his gurney out of the way, his nurse crossed over. She locked her gaze on his and spoke in a low tone. "Derek, the lower lobe of your right lung has collapsed. Dr. Allen needs to put a small catheter in between your ribs to re-inflate your lung."

"Can he do that right here? Or do I have to go to the operating room?" he asked, dreading the answer.

"He can do that right here, but it's going to hurt." Her large chocolate-brown eyes held sympathy.

"Let's get it done fast, then, before Lexi is out of the scanner."

"That's what I thought, too," she confessed. When she leaned closer, her nametag came into focus. Julie. He remembered now, her name was Julie. The pretty name somehow fit her dainty frame and cheerful personality. "I need to prep the side of your chest, first, okay?"

"Go for it," he said. "Just hurry."

She hadn't been kidding about the pain, but surprisingly, once the procedure was over, the fire in his chest felt better. The pain wasn't gone, not by a long shot, but breathing was certainly was easier.

"Now just a quick X-ray of your arm and your chest to make sure your lung has re-inflated, and you'll be set for a while," Julie informed him.

"No other internal bleeding?" he asked. Even though he had no plans of staying, he wanted to know exactly what he was dealing with.

"You have a hard head, but luckily, no sign of intracranial bleeding, although you do have a small concussion. You also have two cracked ribs and a bruised spleen, but no other internal bleeding was found. And Lexi's scan is complete too. Rick, our orderly, is bringing her back here momentarily. Her scan was completely clear. You and your daughter are very lucky to have escaped serious injury."

"Great." The relief was nearly overwhelming. Once he would have thanked God, but not anymore. Not that he thought God would listen to him anyway, considering the way he'd taken Lexi and bolted out of St. Louis in the dead of night. But no matter what, he wasn't going to take Lexi back.

The urge to keep moving was strong. They couldn't afford to stay in one place for too long.

He focused his gaze on Julie. "We are lucky, but we're finished here. I suggest you get our discharge paperwork started, because we're leaving as soon as possible."

2

Derek watched Julie's brown eyes widen in horror. "What? You can't leave, not with a chest catheter in place. We want to keep you overnight, to make sure your concussion doesn't get worse." Her distress was obvious. And maybe, if circumstances had been different, he might have considered staying.

But he needed to protect Lexi.

No matter what.

"I'm not staying here overnight." Slowly, he sat upright on the gurney, mentally prepared this time for the pain slicing through his chest. He swung his legs over the side, hiding the stab of pain the best he could. "Since Lexi's fine, we're leaving. We missed dinner, and I'm sure she's hungry."

To his amazement, Julie planted her hands on her slim hips and stood directly in front of him, staring him down. "Oh, really? And how do you plan on leaving here? On wings? Because from what I heard of the crash, your vehicle isn't drivable."

He momentarily closed his eyes, belatedly remembering that inescapable fact. Okay, so they couldn't drive off to another town, but that didn't mean they had to stay at the hospital. He opened his eyes and focused on Julie. "Where's the nearest motel?"

"Mr. Ryerson, the closest motel is in Crystal Lake, about ten miles away, but it's the height of the tourist season, not to mention Friday night of a holiday weekend. Why don't you just stay here at the hospital for one night? That way, we'll know for sure you're stable enough to leave."

He shook his head. "No thanks. I know my rights—you can't keep me here against my will. I need some clothes. And would you mind if I borrowed your phone? I'd like to call the motel, regardless. Maybe they had a cancellation." The alternative—staying here—was almost too much to bear. He didn't want Lexi to end up in the child welfare system, or worse, with her grandparents again. His daughter was staying with him, end of story.

Julie let out a heavy sigh. "It's easy to see where your daughter gets her stubborn streak."

He ignored the jab, keeping an eye on his daughter, who was staring at him with her usual unblinking gaze. "Lexi, we're going to leave as soon as we sign off on some paperwork, okay?"

She gave another of her tiny nods.

"I have to let Dr. Allen know you're planning to leave AMA," Julie muttered. At his questioning glance, she added, "Against medical advice."

Julie left, and he stayed sitting upright at the edge of the gurney, although he wanted nothing more than to lie back down, because now his head was throbbing in sync with his ribs.

"Daddy." Lexi reached out and put her small hand on his bare knee. "You're hurt."

Sometimes he forgot just how smart his daughter was,

when she hid behind her wall of silence. "Not that bad, baby-doll. I'll be fine, don't worry."

The doctor came into the cubicle, a frown furrowed between his brows. "I hear you're planning to leave AMA."

"Look, Doc, I don't have insurance, and with my daughter here depending on me, I can't afford to stay. So cut me a little slack, would you? Surely it's safe to discharge me."

"Did you forget about the catheter we left between your ribs to keep your lung inflated?" the doctor asked dryly.

Well, yeah, maybe he had. He bit back a surge of impatience. "Okay, how long does the catheter need to stay in?" he asked. "As a former soldier, I know a little about field medicine. I'll pull it out myself in a couple of days."

The doctor scowled but then relented. "Look, I'll agree to discharge you, but on the condition you come back tomorrow, so I can at least look you over one more time. If your lung is good, I'll take the catheter out. No charge," he added hastily when Derek opened his mouth to argue. "A free follow-up visit isn't too much to ask, is it?"

Since Lexi was still watching him with her eerie, unblinking stare, he nodded in agreement, more for her benefit than his. "Sure Doc, no problem. Whatever you say."

"Good." The doctor stared at him for a moment, as if unsure whether or not to trust him. "I'll give you twenty-four hours' worth of narcotics, to hold you over until you can get the prescription filled. Julie will be back soon with your scripts and your discharge paperwork."

He hoped she'd also bring scrubs and a phone, too. He nodded even though all this movement was making his head hurt worse, but he had no intention of giving them any reason to keep him here. If they knew how bad he really felt, they'd prevent him from putting one foot out the door.

Julie didn't come back for a good ten minutes, and when she did, her smile was strained. "There's a deputy who wants to see you before you leave." She set a clean pair of scrubs on the gurney next to him. "Once you're finished with the police, I'll be back with my phone."

Police? He froze, trying to think rationally. The last thing he wanted to do was to talk to the cops. What if they knew about Lexi and hauled him to jail? He didn't have to talk to them, did he? Before he could say anything, Julie disappeared, and a cop strode in.

"Mr. Ryerson? My name is Deputy Thomas. How are you and your daughter feeling?" The deputy looked young, not even close to his thirty, and he found himself hoping that the guy's youth might work in his favor.

"We're fine. Just a bit bruised. What happened to the driver of the pickup truck?"

The deputy scowled. "He's been arrested. I need to ask you a few questions so I can finish up the accident report."

His gut tightened at the thought of answering a bunch of questions. How long before Claire's parents found him? Did they already have an AMBER alert out for Lexi? No, surely not. He was Lexi's legal guardian.

For now.

"I see from your registration that you're from St. Louis, Missouri," Deputy Thomas said. "Whatcha doing way up here in Crystal Lake, Wisconsin?"

He could feel beads of sweat rolling down his spine. "Taking a summer vacation with my daughter," he answered easily. He sensed Lexi moving closer to him, and he put his arms around her slim shoulders. "Friend of mine recommended Crystal Lake."

"Really? Who's your friend?"

He swallowed hard. "Jake Strawn. He lives in Chicago,

and he spent some time up here a few years ago." Jake Strawn had been a soldier in his platoon, and he did live in Chicago. The rest was a slight stretch of the truth.

Deputy Thomas scrunched up his forehead. "Name doesn't ring a bell," he said slowly. For a moment, Derek thought the deputy would see right through him. "But then again, we get lots of tourists up here from Northern Illinois. Probably a good thing his name doesn't sound familiar, right?"

A wave of overwhelming relief almost caused him to fall off the gurney. It took a moment before he could speak. "Can I get a copy of the accident report for my insurance company?"

"Sure, just give us a few days to get everything processed. Might be ready by Monday."

"Thank you." Derek smiled and hoped Deputy Thomas would leave. Soon. Like now.

"Anything else you need?" Thomas asked.

For a moment, he was tempted to ask for a ride but decided it wasn't worth the risk. For all he knew, Claire's parents had already put out the alert. "No, I'm fine."

"Okay, then, take care."

"I will." He held his breath until the deputy had gone. For a moment, he closed his eyes, tempted to say a tiny prayer of thanks.

Except he didn't pray anymore.

"Are you okay?" Julie had returned and was looking at him with concern. He forced another smile, hoping he didn't look nearly as bad as he felt.

"I'm fine."

She held out a slim device. "Here's my mobile phone. I have the number for the Crystal Lake Motel programmed in if you want to call them, but I can already tell you they're booked. And so is every other motel and bed and breakfast within a twenty-mile radius. The Fourth of July is Tuesday, and lots of people are making a long weekend out of the summer holiday."

His heart sank as he took the cell phone. He made the call even though he knew she hadn't been kidding. No vacancies. Within a twenty-mile radius. And he had no car. Maybe he should have taken a ride from the deputy? His shoulders slumped as he tried to figure out their next best option.

Too bad he was all out of ideas.

"Look, Mr. Ryerson," she started.

"Call me Derek," he interrupted.

"Ah, okay, Derek. Please reconsider staying overnight here."

"No can do." He slid off the gurney and reached for the scrubs. "We'll figure out something," he said with more confidence than he felt.

Julie turned away, her expression grim. Abruptly, she spun back to face him. "Look, I own a side-by-side townhouse. I live on one side, and the other side is undergoing major remodeling. But the good news is that the bedrooms are fine; it's the kitchen and living rooms that are pretty much gutted, so you won't be able to cook. But you and your daughter are welcome to stay there, if you don't mind spending the night in the middle of a construction zone."

Was she serious? With a flare of hope, Derek pinned her with an intense gaze. It was then he noticed the slender cross she wore around her neck. She was a Christian, and offering a place to stay for a family in need was exactly something a Christian would do.

His relief was short-lived as he tried not to think about how sweet Julie would turn her back on him in a heartbeat if she knew he was on the run with his daughter. Claire's parents had filed a court order to take custody away from him, and he feared they had the power and the money to succeed. Would Claire's parents file a police report about Lexi missing? Based on the Deputy's response, he thought maybe they hadn't gone to the police, at least not yet. Maybe they would use a private investigator, to keep things quiet.

Either way, Lexi's grandparents wouldn't stop until they got what they wanted. They were rich and entirely too used to getting their own way.

But there would be plenty of time to worry about them in the morning. Right now, he was grateful to know he and Lexi had a safe place to stay. Surely he'd feel better in the morning. "Thanks very much, we'd love to take you up on your generous offer, wouldn't we, Lexi?"

His daughter, as usual, didn't reply but simply stared at him, her bright blue eyes full of concern and a hint of fear.

His gut clenched, and he knew he'd do anything necessary to remove the last remnants of fear from his daughter's eyes.

Anything.

————

FOR A MOMENT, Julie wished she could take back the impulsive offer. You'd think she'd have learned her lesson about getting too involved with a patient after the fiasco with Andrew, but no, here she was putting herself in the middle of Derek's situation. But what else could she do? There really wasn't anywhere else for him to go, and truly, she'd made the offer in the first place for Lexi's sake.

Because of Amelia.

She couldn't, in good conscience, simply let Derek and Lexi walk out the door without a vehicle or a place to stay. She'd just have to make sure she kept her distance emotionally.

She forced a smile. "Okay, give me a few minutes, and we can leave. My shift ended well over an hour ago, so this won't take long. If you need help getting the scrubs on, let me know." She hoped he didn't notice her blush.

"Thanks," he said again. And the genuine sincerity reflected on his face knocked her off balance.

Last year, after the painful disintegration of her engagement, she'd made a conscious effort to avoid men. Which hadn't been too difficult, since there wasn't an overabundance of single men in Crystal Lake.

A fact that had suited her just fine.

Derek Ryerson was a patient, just like Andrew had been. But Derek was different in that he was a father with a young daughter. As soon as Derek was healthy, they'd be on their way to wherever they were headed. Hardly anyone came to Crystal Lake with the intention of staying.

Soon enough, things would go back to normal.

Ignoring her aching feet, she walked to the computer to finish up her charting. Thankfully, Merry had taken care of Lexi's discharge note before she'd left for the evening, so all she had to do was to finish Derek's. After five minutes, she sat back, satisfied she'd completed all the required documentation, and logged off the computer.

When she returned to Derek's room, she noticed he'd managed to get the scrub pants on and the scrub top, too, although he'd hacked at it with a scissor, cutting it down the front so that he didn't have to lift his arms over his head.

The wallet he'd tucked into the front pocket of the scrubs made the fabric hang crooked.

Why his resourcefulness made her want to smile, she had no idea. "Are you both ready?" she asked.

"Sure." He reached over to take Lexi's hand, and she recognized the quick flash of pain that he tried to hide.

"Why don't you both wait out front for me, and I'll drive my car up to the door," she offered. "Save you some walking."

She almost expected him to argue, but he nodded. "Okay. What kind of car do you have?"

"An old green Honda." She left Derek and his daughter standing outside in the cool, summer night and jogged to her car, trying to ignore the screaming protest of the soles of her feet. She reminded herself that her aches and pains were nothing compared to how Derek must feel.

She drove up to the main emergency entrance and found Derek holding Lexi's hand and leaning heavily on a cement pillar. She'd suspected he was hurt far worse than he'd let on.

At least with him staying at her townhouse, she could keep an eye on him. And help take care of his daughter at the same time.

"I don't have a booster seat for Lexi," she pointed out apologetically, opening both the front and back passenger doors. "Luckily, my townhouse isn't far, just ten to fifteen minutes away. She should be fine in the backseat."

"I'll sit in back with her," Derek said, making Lexi scoot over while he carefully lowered himself into the backseat. She noticed that he looked like he was still in pain, but didn't say anything. He'd refused to stay at the hospital, and there was no reason to keep harping on him about it.

She shut the doors and then ran around to the driver's

seat. The silence from the back was a little uncomfortable, so she found herself chatting idly as she headed toward home. "Crystal Lake is a spring-fed lake, about six miles wide and nine miles long. It's very peaceful at night, but during the day there's lots of activity—boaters, water-skiers, wave runners, and inner-tubers."

She glanced in the rearview mirror, not entirely surprised to find Derek with his head back against the seat and his eyes closed. Lexi was wide awake, though, staring straight ahead, possibly listening, although she didn't say anything.

"I don't know if you've ever been inner-tubing, Lexi, but it's great fun. You sit in the middle of an inner tube, and a boat pulls you around the lake. If you and your dad plan on staying for a few days, maybe we can try it."

Lexi blinked and gave a tiny nod. Julie frowned, thinking the young girl was unusually quiet for a six-year-old. Amelia had talked nonstop, asking dozens of questions, ever curious.

Until a rare form of leukemia had taken her young life.

Her chest constricted, and she shoved thoughts of her niece out of her mind. Even after eighteen months, the memories sneaked up on her, blindsiding her with their potency.

"Your dad mentioned something about food. We can stop for a pizza on the way home," she offered. "Do you like pizza? Or do you want something else?"

There was a long pause, and this time Lexi answered in a soft voice. "Pizza."

Derek roused himself, giving his daughter a nudge. "What do you say, Lexi?"

There was a slight pause. "Please."

"Okay, pizza it is." She smiled at Derek in the rearview mirror. "I thought you were asleep."

"No, just resting."

Belatedly, she remembered the prescription for pain medication. "I should stop at the pharmacy first, so we can get your prescription filled."

"No need. The doc gave me a few samples. I should be fine until tomorrow."

She wasn't surprised Gabe had given him some free meds, since he'd mentioned Derek's lack of health insurance. She wondered if Derek had enough money to get the prescription filled.

There was a pizza place in town that sold pre-made cheese pizzas for five bucks each. She bought two and then headed home.

Her townhouse was on the outskirts of town, overlooking the lake. The place had been partially destroyed by a kitchen fire, and the former owners, who lived in Illinois, had sold it to her at a steep discount. Julie was hoping she could eventually fix it up and either rent out the one half for a little additional income or potentially sell it, depending on what happened with the real estate market.

After almost two years, though, she wasn't nearly as far along on the remodeling as she'd hoped to be. Partially because sinks, commodes, counters, and cabinets cost far more than she ever would have imagined. And she'd also have to pay someone to help her install the new items, which would cut deeply into her meager savings.

She'd spent most of the first year making her side more livable and had only recently started on the other side.

"Here we are," she said brightly, as she pulled into the driveway of the unoccupied side of the townhouse. The layouts of the two townhouses were mirror images of each other. In the back, there were patio doors from both kitchens leading out to a cement slab, where she had some secondhand patio furniture. "Lexi, will you carry the pizzas while I help your dad?"

The girl wordlessly took the boxes she gently placed in her arms, while Derek tried to maneuver his way out of the backseat on his own.

"Stubborn man," she muttered half under her breath as she went around to the passenger side to give a helping hand. "Let me help," she advised. "If you pass out on me, I'll never get you inside by myself."

"I won't pass out," he said, his voice low and raw with pain and determination.

She didn't bother to point out the obvious, that he might not have much choice in the matter. She ducked her head inside the car and hooked her left arm beneath his right armpit. "Grab on to the car frame with your good arm," she directed. "On the count of three, we're going to swing you out. Ready?" He nodded, and she braced herself with her right arm on the car the best she could, as well. "One, two, *three!*"

They both pulled, hauling him to his feet. Derek groaned, sagging against the car as if his legs wouldn't hold him up. She held on to him, pressing him back against the car, hoping he wouldn't fall.

"Are you all right?" she asked, glancing up at his face, which was disconcertingly close.

"Yes." His voice sounded weak, thready. "Give me...a...minute."

"Take as much time as you need." He was too big, too heavy for her to do much else. She needed him to be able to get into the house under his own power. She glanced over at Lexi, who was staring at them both with her wide eyes. "Are you hungry, Lexi? Because I sure am, and that pizza smells really good."

Derek opened his eyes and straightened, as she suspected he would the moment she mentioned Lexi. Derek's strength when it came to his daughter was nothing short of amazing. "I'm hungry, too," he said in a forced tone. "Let's get settled inside so we can eat."

Once she ascertained he was actually supporting his own weight, she slowly moved away. She went around and opened the front door, using her key. She flipped on the living room lights, wincing a little at how awful the walls looked. In some areas, the blackened drywall was still in place, and in others, the drywall had been stripped away, revealing bare studs and electrical wires. She held the door open for Lexi and Derek.

"I told you it was under construction," she said defensively when he glanced around curiously.

"It's fine," he said gruffly. "Are there beds, or are we sleeping on the floor?"

She was impressed he'd even considered sleeping on the floor, considering his cracked ribs. "There are twin beds in the first bedroom, but I'll have to run over to get sheets. I'll pick up some paper plates and napkins, too. The water still works in the bathrooms but not in the kitchen. I'll turn up the hot water heater for you. And there isn't a stove or fridge." She knew it was ridiculous, but she felt bad she didn't have more to offer him. She was almost tempted to give him her side, but even though he was injured, he was a stranger. And besides, she could just as easily provide them some meals without giving up her personal space.

"This is perfect," Derek said as he made his way down the hall to the closest bedroom. He went straight toward the side of the bed and eased his weight on the edge of the mattress. It was as if he'd read her mind when he continued, "I can't thank you enough for providing us a place to sleep."

She flashed a small smile, trying to convince herself she was not making the same mistakes she'd made with Andrew, as she took the pizza boxes from Lexi and set them on the small bedside table between the two beds. "I'll be right back," she promised.

Out in the kitchen, she opened the patio doors and went over to her side of the townhouse. She didn't bother to lock her patio doors as there was hardly any crime in Crystal Lake.

She found two sets of sheets, two lightweight blankets, and a couple of spare pillows in her linen closet. Back in the kitchen, her heart jumped into her throat when she found Lexi standing there, staring at her.

"Did you come to help?" she asked, even though she knew by now not to expect an answer. "Here, you can carry the paper plates, paper cups, and napkins, okay?"

Lexi obediently took the items and then went back out through the patio doors to return to the side where her father waited. Julie followed more slowly, stepping carefully since she couldn't see very well around the bundle of bedding in her arms.

While Derek stood up, she quickly made the beds, working as fast as possible so he could sit back down. He didn't eat much, but Lexi devoured her pizza, betraying the depth of her hunger.

Derek's face was pale, and she suspected he was staying upright by sheer stubborn will. Chatting with Lexi, Julie cleaned up the napkins and paper plates and then picked up the leftover pizza. "I'll keep this in my fridge. If you need anything, I'm right next door, okay?" The nurse in her didn't want to leave, and suddenly she was worried about Lexi. "Maybe Lexi should stay with me?" she offered.

Lexi moved closer to her father, and Derek put his arm around her shoulders. "We'll be just fine, won't we, Lexi?"

"All right," she agreed, knowing that rest would likely help Derek more than anything else. "Take your medicine, okay?"

"I already did. Thank you," Derek said again.

She nodded and slipped out of the townhouse through the patio doors in the demolished kitchen, leaving father and daughter alone.

The hour wasn't all that late, just nine fifteen, but she was exhausted, so she didn't waste any time heading to bed. When a strange sound woke her up, she gasped and peered through the darkness. It took a moment to realize the small face peering at her belonged to Lexi.

"What's wrong?" she asked.

"Help my daddy," Lexi said, her gaze intense. "Please, help my daddy!"

3

Derek groaned under his breath and pulled himself across the hallway floor, beads of sweat rolling freely down his face, burning his eyes.

The plank-wood floor had plenty of splintered edges, but he ignored the minor irritation. He knew he'd frightened Lexi, and his mission right now was to get back into the bedroom, where he could possibly use the bed frame as leverage to get back up.

Get up, soldier! Now! No excuses! You're a soldier, so you'd better start acting like one!

Derek used his legs and his good arm to propel his body across the floor, inch by agonizing inch, finally crossing the threshold into the bedroom. The fire was back in his chest, worse than before, and he suspected that he'd inadvertently displaced the catheter they'd stuck in his chest to re-inflate his lung.

"Lexi?" he called out, unsure where his daughter had gone. "I'm here and I'm fine. I'm going to get into bed, now, see?"

Actually, he couldn't see a thing through the red haze of pain that shrouded his vision.

He grasped the lower bed frame and tried to figure out how to pull himself upright. He closed his eyes, thinking it would be easier to stay on the floor. He'd ask Lexi to give him a pillow, and he'd be fine until morning.

"Derek, are you okay?"

He recognized that soft, female voice. Julie. The nurse. He forced his eyelids open.

Nothing worse than feeling helpless, especially when he realized Lexi had woken her up. Because of him.

"Derek? What happened?" she asked.

She touched his shoulder, and he shoved his lame pride aside to answer. He couldn't read the expression on her face with the hallway light on behind her. "Sneezed. Woke up on the bathroom floor."

"You passed out?" Instantly, she dropped to her knees, bringing her face closer to his. "Did you hit your head again?"

"No." At least he didn't think so. The pain in his head was about the same; it was his chest that was killing him. He didn't like being dependent on her for help. Didn't like being dependent on anyone other than himself. "Toss me a pillow and a blanket. I'll rest here until morning."

"Don't be ridiculous," she said, and he heard the distinct note of impatience in her tone. "You're not sleeping on the floor. If I can't help you up, I'll call an ambulance."

"No ambulance." Since she was obviously going to be difficult about this, he rolled onto his injured side and grabbed on to the bed frame with his uninjured left arm. "I'll get up."

She muttered something under her breath that he

couldn't quite make out. It sounded like stubborn as an ox, but he couldn't bring himself to care. She put her arm under his right armpit again. "Try just sitting first. Your legs are strong. Once we get you into a sitting position, you should be able to stand."

Easy for her to say—her rib cage wasn't engulfed in fire. His lungs felt like two strips of sandpaper rubbing together with every breath. But complaining didn't get the job done, so he concentrated on pushing off the bed frame. With Julie adding her strength and supporting his injured side, he suddenly found himself sitting upright, his side pressed against the bed.

"Thanks," he grunted, trying to catch his breath. But it was no use. That stupid catheter wasn't keeping his lung inflated, and the last thing he wanted to do was to go back to the hospital. For sure, they'd keep him.

And he didn't think he had the strength to leave AMA a second time.

"Rest for a minute, and then I'll help you get up on your feet," she said, her voice close to his ear.

He had the absurd thought that, with Julie's support, he could do anything.

He glanced over at Lexi, who stood silently, her eyes wide and her face pale. He forced himself to smile for her benefit. "I'm proud of you, Lexi. You were smart to get help."

His words didn't seem to reassure his daughter, so he decided the only thing that was going to make Lexi feel better was if he could get up on his feet and back on top of the bed.

"Use the strength in your legs as much as you can," Julie advised when she felt him shift. "I'll give you as much leverage as I can manage."

Considering she was all of five foot three inches on a good day and weighed, in his estimation, less than a hundred and twenty pounds, he couldn't imagine she'd provide any leverage. Although she'd surprised him with her ability to get him out of the backseat of the car.

Maybe being close to God gave her an edge over everyone else. Right now, he'd use any advantage he could get.

He leaned against the bed frame, trying to get his legs into a good position. Between support from the bed frame and Julie's help, he somehow managed to get his feet under him, and finally, he was up and sitting on the edge of the bed.

The pressure on his chest didn't ease, and he struggled to breathe. Something so natural shouldn't be so difficult.

A cold, round circle was pressed against his side, and he realized Julie had a stethoscope in her ears, listening to his chest. "Your lung is down again," she said accusingly, as if he'd done the deed on purpose.

"I know," was all he could manage. What did she want him to say? The sneeze had caught him off guard, and the pain had been so intense he'd dropped like a stone.

"Stay sitting upright. I'm going to try something, okay?"

He nodded, since he wasn't in any shape to stop her anyway.

She bent down and sucked on the end of the pigtail catheter hanging out of his chest, like she was drinking a thick malt out of a straw. And suddenly, the fire eased, and he could breathe again.

"It worked," he said in amazement. He took another breath, just to make sure his imagination hadn't played tricks on him. "I can breathe easier."

"There's a valve in these catheters, which must have closed when you sneezed." She peered down at the dressing around the catheter, no doubt looking for signs of bleeding.

"Well, that settles it, no more sneezing for me," he said in an attempt to lighten the mood. He reached out a hand toward his daughter, who came over to huddle next to him. He hugged her reassuringly. "I'm fine, Lexi. Thanks to Julie, I'm going to be just fine."

Julie stared at him, clearly exasperated. "I suppose I'd be wasting my breath if I encouraged you to go back to the hospital."

For a moment, he almost felt guilty for disappointing her. "Yes, because there's no need to go back. I'm fine now. Thanks for your help. Again."

"Stop thanking me," she said suddenly, scrubbing her hands over her face. "This is my fault. I should have offered you my place to spend the night. I should have thought about the drywall dust making you sneeze."

The way she was beating herself up over something she couldn't control was ridiculous. "Don't, Julie. You've gone out of your way to offer us a place to stay. I'm very grateful. Besides, it probably wasn't the drywall dust that made me sneeze. I have allergies." A small stretch of the truth. He was only allergic to cats, and even though he hadn't seen any, it didn't mean she didn't have one tucked away somewhere.

She stared at him for a few minutes, as if she didn't believe in his allergies for one minute, before she finally turned away. "I'll get you another dose of pain medicine, and then you really need to try and get some rest."

"What time is it?" he asked when she brought over two pills and a glass of water. He didn't think he was due for more pain meds yet.

"One thirty in the morning. And don't worry, you can take the medication every four hours."

He gratefully swallowed the pills and then kissed the top of Lexi's head before easing himself down on the bed. "Okay, baby-doll, it's time to get some sleep."

Lexi obediently climbed into her twin bed but lay on her side, right near the edge, facing him. Her eyes were wide open, almost as if she were afraid to fall asleep.

His heart squeezed in his chest. His poor daughter had been through so much. He wanted desperately to give Lexi the solid foundation of love and support she needed.

That she deserved.

"Goodnight, Lexi. Goodnight, Derek," Julie said as she headed back out to the hall.

Before Derek could answer, he was shocked and stunned beyond words to hear his daughter reply in a soft voice, "Goodnight, Julie."

———————

THE NEXT MORNING, Julie crawled out of bed far later than normal, thankful that she had the next three days off work.

Remembering her overnight guests staying next door spurred her into action. Derek hadn't eaten much pizza last night; he was undoubtedly hungry.

After she showered and dressed, she headed into the kitchen to prepare breakfast. Cooking for guests seemed strange. Not that Derek was really a guest. He was more like a patient.

Best to remember that fact. The sooner he felt better, the sooner he and Lexi would be on their way.

She needed to keep her distance from Derek and Lexi. Getting emotionally involved would only result in feeling hurt when it was time for them to move on. Yet she couldn't deny that Lexi's soft goodnight had touched her deep in her heart, the effect lingering long after she'd returned to her side of the townhouse.

Lexi reminded her of Amelia, even though the two girls were as different as night and day. Lexi was far too quiet, although maybe the trauma of being in a crash, on top of having her father injured, had been too much for the little girl to handle.

The summer heat was already making the interior of her kitchen stuffy, even with the open windows, so she made sure every ceiling fan was on to help circulate the air. By mid afternoon, she might have to use the air conditioner, although she'd rather not.

As she cooked a big batch of scrambled eggs, she wondered about Lexi's mother. Not once during their brief stay in the ER, or last night for that matter, did the little girl ask for her mother. Only her father.

Had Derek tragically lost his wife? Or were they divorced? Either option must have been a while ago, or surely Lexi would have called out for her mother when she arrived in the trauma bay.

She plunked the toast into the toaster then turned back to check the eggs and nearly shrieked when she saw Lexi hovering near the patio doors.

Obviously she'd been so preoccupied with thoughts of Derek that she hadn't heard the child come in.

Putting a hand over her racing heart, she forced a smile. "Good morning, Lexi. I'm cooking breakfast for you and your dad. Do you like scrambled eggs? If not, I have Cheerios and milk."

Lexi stared at her solemnly for so long Julie didn't think she'd answer. "Eggs."

"Great, scrambled eggs it is. Did you come over to help? That's very nice." Then she frowned. "Unless, there's something you need? Is your dad all right?"

Lexi did that tiny nod that, if Julie wasn't watching closely enough, she might have missed. "I'm hungry."

"Me too." The toast popped, so she spread a thin layer of butter over the crispy browned bread. "Do you want to help me carry this over to your dad?" She glanced at her kitchen table and abruptly changed her mind. "You know what, Lexi? It would be easier to eat in my kitchen. Let's ask your dad to come over here."

Lexi darted out the patio door without answering, and Julie had to assume that she'd gone to get her father. It was tempting to go over to offer Derek assistance, but she purposely held herself back.

If Derek wasn't able to stand and walk over here to sit at the kitchen table for a simple meal, then he needed to be taken back to the hospital, despite his protests.

But she needn't have worried. Lexi soon returned with her father on her heels. Wearing the same scrubs she'd given him last night, he moved slowly and gingerly but held himself straight and tall.

"Good morning," she greeted them both cheerfully, trying not to hover as Derek eased himself into a chair. "Hope scrambled eggs and toast is okay." Why the sudden rush of nervousness? She wasn't running a restaurant, and he was hardly in a position to argue about what she fed him.

The un-Christian thought shamed her.

"Sounds better than okay," Derek said quickly. For being injured, he seemed acutely aware of her emotions. Or maybe she just wasn't good at hiding them. "Lexi loves scrambled eggs, don't you, sweetheart?"

Lexi nodded and then ducked her head, swinging her legs back and forth in a steady rhythm. Julie gave Lexi the first plate of food, Derek the second, and then went back to get something for herself.

Once seated, she bowed her head and clasped her hands together. "Dear Lord, thank you for this plentiful meal we're about to eat. Please help Derek get better soon and guide us on Your chosen path as we begin our day. Amen."

A brief silence followed her prayer, and she could feel the intensity of Derek's curious gaze as she took a bite of her eggs. Hadn't he ever witnessed anyone praying before? Or prayed for him to get better? If not, his education was sorely lacking.

"How are you feeling today?" she asked, glancing at Derek.

"As good as can be expected," he admitted. "Surprisingly, the pain seems a bit better when I'm up and moving."

"Your muscles will become stiff and sore if you stay in one place too long. As difficult as I'm sure it must be, you need to keep moving."

He flashed a smile and nodded. "Good advice, Nurse Julie."

She could feel herself blushing and focused her attention on her food.

"Sure is peaceful around here," Derek said, staring through the screen to the concrete patio.

"Yes, I love the peace and quiet." She had a small television but didn't turn it on often. Sometimes she listened to the national news, but lately, the global turmoil was just too depressing. "Would you rather listen to the radio?"

"No." The force of his abrupt response surprised her. "I like the peace and quiet, too."

Such a small thing in common, yet it made her smile inside. "So, what are your plans for the day?"

He stared at his plate for a moment. "I have to find out the extent of the damage to my car. I'm not even sure it's fixable. And the doc wanted to check me over one more time." She was pleased he finished up his eggs and started on the toast. At least his appetite seemed to have returned. "I know I have no right to ask any more favors," he said in a low voice. "But would you mind giving us a ride? If you have the day off, that is."

"Yes, I have the next couple of days off. And of course I don't mind giving you a ride." She told herself that spending the day with Derek and Lexi was nothing like what had happened with Andrew, but it was. Andrew had needed her help, just like Derek. Her own fault for believing Andrew cared about her in return.

She'd just have to make sure she didn't get too emotionally involved with Derek and Lexi.

But even if she had thought things through last evening, she knew she would have made the same offer.

Where else would Derek and Lexi have gone?

"Thank you," Derek murmured. "If all the people here are as gracious and kind as you, Crystal Lake must be a wonderful place to live."

"Crystal Lake is a great place to live, and anyone here would have done the same thing I did." She stood and began stacking the dirty dishes to carry them over to the counter. "You'll have to give me a few minutes to clean up before I'll be ready to go."

He glanced at the dishes on the counter. "I'll help," he offered.

Whoever this stranger was, he was certainly polite. "Really, it's easier if I wash them myself." She couldn't explain why the thought of standing next to Derek, doing something as mundane as dishes, made her distinctly uncomfortable.

There was a brief pause, and then he capitulated. "All right, then. Come on Lexi, let's go over and make our beds, okay?"

When the screen door slammed behind them, she put her hands on the counter and momentarily closed her eyes.

Why was she so attracted to Derek? Okay, maybe Derek was strong, kind, gentle, and polite—seemingly everything Andrew had proved he wasn't. So what? She should be glad she'd offered her townhouse to a nice stranger.

Just as she was glad she'd found out about Andrew's lying and cheating before she'd vowed to love, honor, and cherish him.

Derek and Lexi were only passing through town. Or looking to spend some quiet time together. She refused to entertain the hope that Derek Ryerson and his young daughter would stay to make a home here in Crystal Lake.

———

DEREK FOUGHT a wave of guilt as he helped Lexi straighten the sheet and blanket on her bed. He knew he was taking advantage of Julie's sweet, Christian nature, but what choice did he have?

He was glad the news of his and Lexi's disappearance didn't seem to have made its way to the small town of Crystal Lake, Wisconsin. But how long did he have before the alarm went out? Thanks to the Fourth of July holiday on Tuesday, he likely had a couple of days to figure out their next steps before he had to go on the run again.

Claire's parents couldn't serve him a court order if they couldn't find him.

He tried to consider his options, but there weren't many. The last thing he wanted to do was to betray Julie by stealing her car. A fleeting thought that had crossed his mind. The problem was that he only had a couple of thousand in cash, and he couldn't afford to spend it all in one place.

He'd need something to tide them over until he could find a job. Especially with the economy as bad as it was. Most of his experience was as a soldier and even though he'd received an honorable discharge there was no guarantee he'd find something quickly or easily.

Once he and Lexi had made the twin beds, he wandered back into the half-demolished, open-concept kitchen and living area. There was a crowbar propped against the wall that still had some charred Sheetrock hanging.

Julie was clearly working on her remodeling project a little at a time. Pulling down old drywall didn't take a whole lot of finesse, but putting up new Sheetrock did. Luckily, he had some experience with construction work.

He lifted the crowbar, wincing as the muscles in his chest protested. Steeling himself against the pain, he drove the claw end of the crowbar into the seared drywall and pulled, bringing a big chunk of drywall crashing to the floor.

He sucked in a quick breath. Yeah, that hurt. But so what? As he lifted the crowbar, intending to take another chunk of the wall down, an idea burned in his mind.

Julie yanked open the screen door and glared at him.

"What's going on?" she demanded. "You scared me to death, making all that noise."

"Sorry," he said with a grimace. He leaned the crowbar back up against the wall and shifted to face her. "I found a way to repay you for your generosity." He lifted a hand, indicating the room. "I'll work on your remodeling project as payment for you allowing me and Lexi to stay here for the next few days."

4

J ulie stared at Derek in shock. His offer was generous, but really, she couldn't believe he was even considering doing physical work on her town-house while having cracked ribs. The man was truly a glutton for punishment. "Derek, there's no need for you to worry about paying me back. You can't do construc-tion work until you're medically cleared by the doctor."

His smile was pained. "I'm a former Army sergeant. I assure you I can work on the townhouse just fine. And don't worry, I know my limits. I won't overdo things. But I can still help out."

Had she ever met a more stubborn man? She bit back a surge of frustration. "Let's get to the hospital, okay? We have plenty of other things to do right now rather than wasting time arguing over this."

"Please," he said in a low voice.

Her annoyance faded at the softly spoken plea. She understood that being helpless and at other people's mercy was probably difficult for him. She wasn't surprised that he was former military, considering the short haircut and the way he carried himself so straight and tall. Once again, she found herself wondering about Lexi's mother. Derek said he and Lexi were alone, but she couldn't help wondering about the woman who'd given birth to Lexi. Not that Derek's loss was any of her business.

She glanced at Lexi, who stared at her with a steady gaze, identical to Derek's. She sighed, knowing she may as well give in since he'd try to do the work anyway. With any luck, he'd get tired quickly. "When you're able to work, I'd be more than happy to work out a deal with you. But first, we're going to see the doctor and check out your car."

"Thank you," he murmured, and she knew the battle had already been lost. Or in his case, won. Not that she planned on keeping score.

They headed outside to where she'd left her car in the driveway. She opened the driver's side door but then stopped when she realized Derek had remained standing over by the townhouse. "Shouldn't we lock the door?" he asked.

"This is Crystal Lake," she said dryly. "We don't lock our doors here."

He looked surprised, making her think that he was used to living in the city rather than in a small town. It made her a little uneasy that there was so much she didn't know about him.

"Would you mind if we went to find my truck first?" he asked as they made their way down the sidewalk to the car. "I'd like to get Lexi's booster seat. And if you're right about the lack of crime around here, maybe our luggage, my phone, and my tools are still inside."

"Sure." She was struck by how Derek always seemed to put his daughter first. He was still a stranger, but he seemed so genuine. Of course, she'd thought the best of Andrew, too, and he'd proved to be a lying, cheating jerk. Obviously she couldn't trust her instincts. At least, not when it came to men.

As before, Derek slid into the backseat to stay near his daughter. She felt like a taxi driver as she maneuvered her way through the small town. This time, Derek looked around curiously rather than being half out of it.

"How did you know my truck would be here?" Derek asked when she pulled up in front of Billy's garage.

"Because Billy's is the only towing service we have," she said, sliding out from behind the wheel. She knew Derek and Lexi followed as she walked over to the open garage door. "Henry! Are you here?"

"His name isn't Billy?" Derek asked, his blue eyes mirroring his confusion.

She laughed. "No, Henry bought the place about ten years ago from old Billy Colby and decided there was no reason to change the name."

"You've lived here a long time, then?" he asked.

Her smile faded. "Yes, I grew up here." Her parents had passed away several years ago, but she never had the urge to leave. Granted, staying on after breaking off her engagement was the hardest thing she'd ever done. At least now that a year had passed, the gossip had died down a bit. Andrew's decision to leave with his new fiancée had helped. She shook off the painful memories. "Henry!"

"I'm right here. Ya don't have to shout." Henry looked older than his forty-five years, thanks to years of smoking. He'd finally quit but constantly chomped on pieces of nicotine gum. He swiped his greasy hands on his coveralls and squinted at them. "Are ya here for the Blazer?"

"Yes. How much do I owe you for the tow?" Derek asked, stepping forward.

"A hundred even," Henry said. "I checked it out, and I gotta tell ya, there ain't no way to salvage it. Probably totaled."

"Where is the vehicle?" she asked as Derek pulled out his wallet. She'd been about to pay the fee herself, but clearly Derek had this covered.

"Around back," Henry said, gesturing with his thumb as he accepted the cash.

She followed the men around the corner and then sucked in a harsh breath, glad she'd lagged behind when she saw what was left of Derek's car.

It was a miracle he wasn't hurt worse. The entire driver's side of the car was nothing but mangled metal. She gave another silent prayer of thanks to God for keeping him safe.

Derek's expression was grim as he went over to the passenger side of the car and opened the door. When he pulled out Lexi's booster seat, she reached around to take it from him.

"I'll put this in my car," she said.

Derek nodded before turning back to the vehicle. She could have assured him that whatever he had in the truck was still there. Henry would never have considered stealing from one of his towed vehicles.

The people of Crystal Lake were generally law-abiding citizens. Especially now that Tommy Hinkle and his father, Kurt, were behind bars.

By the time she'd strapped Lexi's car seat into the back-seat and returned to the mangled car, she discovered that Derek had pulled two suitcases out. The sight of his luggage brought her up short. Was she crazy to allow this man to stay with her? If Andrew were still around, he'd have a fit. But Andrew wasn't part of her life any longer, and despite her unease, she refused to go back on her word.

Hiding her attack of nerves, she picked up the larger of the two suitcases and carried it to her trunk.

Derek carried the smaller suitcase over and stored it beside the larger one. "I'm just going to get my tools," he said before striding back to his wrecked truck.

Within ten minutes, Derek had everything stashed in the back of her car. He went over and said something to Henry. The older man nodded and then shook Derek's hand.

She refrained from asking what transpired despite her curiosity. Derek helped Lexi get into the booster seat and then surprised her by climbing into the passenger seat beside her.

"Next stop, Hope County Hospital," she said cheerfully as she left Billy's garage.

Derek nodded but still looked upset about leaving his truck behind. He fiddled with his phone, sliding the charger into the port and making sure the device still worked.

"You might want to call your insurance company," she said. "The sooner you put them on notice, the sooner they'll cut you a check."

"Yeah." Derek scrubbed his hands over his face. "But I doubt they'll do much without the accident report."

He was right; she should have thought about that. "We can swing by after you've been seen at the hospital," she offered. "May as well get everything done in one trip."

"No need. The deputy told me the report wouldn't be done until Monday," he said.

"I have connections at the sheriff's department. Sheriff Torretti is a great guy and I know his wife Megan. I can ask for a rush on the report."

"Monday is fine," Derek said sharply. When she glanced at him in surprise, he seemed to backpedal. "It's not like anything is going to be processed over the weekend anyway."

She shrugged and let the matter drop. Maybe he was hurting more than he'd let on. Especially after the way he'd been hauling suitcases around.

The sooner Gabe Allen looked him over, the better.

————

DEREK GRIPPED the armrest of the passenger door, hoping Julie wouldn't insist on stopping at the police station. He was thankful she didn't have the news on, but if Claire's parents had put out the alarm, the risk of being arrested was too high. Claire's parents had tons of money, and they'd made it clear that they'd take custody of Lexi away from him.

He tried to take deep, calming breaths, but it wasn't easy with sore ribs. When Julie pulled up in front of the hospital, he gave a tiny sigh of relief.

"Why don't you get out here, and I'll park the car?" she suggested.

"I can walk, you know," he muttered, getting really sick of being treated like an invalid. He supposed that being a nurse made her more conscientious than others, but still. He glanced back at Lexi. "Do you want to come with me?" he asked.

Lexi nodded. He was impressed at how well his daughter was handling all this, especially since she didn't normally warm up to strangers at all. He opened the back passenger door and helped her get out of the booster seat. He lifted Lexi out and then set her on her feet. Before closing the door, he caught Julie's gaze. "Ah, Dr. Allen, right?"

She smiled, and he was surprised at how much that small gesture transformed her features. Julie was really quite pretty in a girl-next-door kind of way. Not as classically beautiful as Claire, but then again, that hadn't worked so well for him, had it? Julie was attractive, but it didn't matter, since he had no plans to stay in Crystal Lake.

He figured he had a week at the most before he needed to be on the road again.

"Yes, Dr. Gabe Allen. Just keep in mind that you might have to wait if they're busy."

"I understand. Thanks again. Come on, Lexi." He took his daughter's hand and walked inside the emergency department. At least this time, he was walking in and not being wheeled in on a gurney.

He told the nurse at the front desk that he was here to see Dr. Allen. She placed the call and, within five minutes, waved him back. "You can go into room three," she directed.

At first, he'd assumed that the ER wasn't very busy since they'd taken him right away, but when he went back into the main arena, he was greeted by a cacophony of activity. Various patients were wailing in pain or yelling out for one reason or another. Monitors beeped, and there seemed to be a constant stream of chatter from the staff who scurried from one place to another.

Room three looked to be one of the few empty rooms, and he felt guilty for wasting the doctor's valuable time. He waited inside the doorway, thinking it might be better if he just left, since they were so busy. Only the thought of disappointing Julie kept him there.

Ten minutes later, Dr. Allen and a nurse rushed in. "So,

how did you survive the night?" the doctor asked without wasting time exchanging small talk.

"Fine," Derek said, lifting his arm so that the nurse could take down the dressing around the chest tube.

"He sneezed, and his lung deflated again," Julie said as she entered the room. "I applied negative pressure on the valve, and he seemed to be better after that."

"Hmmm." The doctor cocked an eyebrow at him questioningly so he reluctantly nodded.

"Yeah, that sounds right."

"We'll need to get another chest X-ray," Dr. Allen said to the nurse. "I'm tempted to leave the catheter in for another day, but we'll see how your X-ray looks."

He kept his mouth shut, sensing it would do no good to argue. When it came time to get the X-ray, he flashed Lexi a reassuring smile before following the nurse to the radiology area.

Five minutes later, he was back in the room. Dr. Allen pulled up the X-ray on the computer screen right in the room. "No sign of the pneumothorax," he muttered. "But I'd still like to keep the catheter in another day."

"I'll bring him back tomorrow after church," Julie said.

Dr. Allen nodded. "I'm not working, but maybe I can just stop by your place. How do your ribs feel?"

"Sore, but tolerable."

"All right, try not to do any more sneezing, and I'll see you tomorrow."

"Thanks Doc," he said, sincerely grateful to know he hadn't made anything worse last night. The pain had been scary, but he felt a hundred percent better today. Well, maybe that was a slight exaggeration. More like fifty percent better. "I appreciate the special treatment."

"No problem." Dr. Allen flashed them both a tired grin before leaving them alone.

Derek held Lexi's hand as he followed Julie back out to the parking lot. Getting in and out of the car still hurt, but he bit back a low groan when he slid inside.

Neither one of them said anything as Julie pulled out of the hospital parking lot.

"The drugstore is on the way home," she said, finally breaking the silence. "We can stop to get your prescription filled."

"I don't need more pain meds," he said quickly. He was afraid if she knew how low he was on cash, she'd insist on paying for them herself, and he was in debt to her enough already. "I still have a couple of the samples left, and I don't plan to use them unless I'm desperate."

"Like you were last night?" she asked. "I can't believe you weren't going to tell the doctor what happened."

He shrugged, feeling guilty for disappointing her when, really, he had far bigger issues to worry about. "You heard the doc, no sign of a pneumo-whatever, so I'm fine."

She didn't answer but tightened her fingers on the steering wheel as if she was struggling not to lose control. He felt bad for making her upset, but he couldn't explain how important it was that he stay out of the hospital at all cost. He didn't want Lexi to end up in the foster care system. And he for sure didn't want Claire's parents to get custody of Lexi again.

Lexi was...special. She didn't need that private super strict school that Claire's parents had picked out for her. Lexi hated it, and forcing her to go was making her worse instead of better. Claire's parents thought she needed structure, but what Lexi needed was love and attention. What she needed was to be with her father and time to recuperate from losing her mother.

Now that he was honorably discharged from the Army, he could take better care of Lexi than a bunch of strangers, no matter how well intentioned.

He'd made a promise to Lexi and to Claire before she died, and he intended to keep it.

5

Julie stood in her kitchen, watching through the patio doors as Derek and Lexi walked down to the lake. Despite her protests, Derek had insisted on bringing in the luggage and his tools. They way he was moving slowly and carefully, favoring his right side, convinced her that he'd overexerted himself. Again. Yet no matter how many times she told him to rest, he ignored her and did what he wanted. Lexi instinctively stayed close to her father's side rather than running toward the water the way Amelia used to do.

Thoughts of her niece always brought the threat of tears, so she turned away, trying to think of other things. It was close to noon, and there was plenty of leftover pizza to eat for lunch, but she also needed something to make for dinner. She opened her freezer and stared at the meager contents.

Hamburgers on the grill sounded good, and best of all, she wouldn't have to turn on her oven. Thanks to her small garden, she even had the fixings for a salad. Tomorrow, after church, she'd have to make a run to the grocery store since she wasn't used to feeding three people.

The sound of boat engines and shrieking laughter filtered in off the lake. Her brother, Zack, left his boat here during the summer months, and she wondered if Derek and Lexi would like to take a spin out on the lake after they'd eaten.

Or maybe they just wanted to spend some time alone. After all, it wasn't her job to entertain them.

No matter how much she wanted to.

Since she was becoming far too fascinated with her unexpected houseguests, she busied herself with doing some bills and other paperwork until her stomach rumbled. Figuring Derek and Lexi must be hungry too, she pulled the leftover pizza out of the fridge and heated it up in her microwave. Then she piled paper plates and napkins on top of the pizza box before making her way outside.

"Are you guys hungry?" she called. "There's plenty of left-over pizza for lunch."

Derek looked up and flashed a smile, which somehow made him look about ten years younger. She wasn't at all happy that her pulse jumped in response. "I am," he said eagerly. "How about it, baby-doll?"

Lexi gave another of her short nods and readily walked back up to the townhouse with her father.

"Thanks, Julie, this looks great," Derek said, looking down at the food with appreciation.

She ducked her head, hoping he hadn't noticed her pink cheeks. Why was she reacting to Derek like this? Ridiculous. "It's nothing, just more leftovers than I could ever finish by myself."

Lexi scrambled up to sit on her knees so she could reach

the table, and Derek gingerly sank into a chair beside her. Julie took her seat and bowed her head to pray.

"Dear Lord, thank You for providing this food and for this fantastic summer day. Amen."

She opened her eyes and looked up, surprised to see that both Derek and Lexi had bowed their heads, too, while she'd prayed. All she knew about Derek was that he used to be in the military, and while he hadn't joined her in prayer, he hadn't scoffed at her faith, either.

And why did she care one way or the other? She had to stop thinking that Derek and Lexi would be here long enough for it to matter. She was simply helping him out of a jam—it wasn't as if this was some sort of long-term friendship or anything.

"Is that boat on the lift yours?" Derek asked before taking a healthy bite of his pizza. He truly looked so much better today that she could barely reconcile this man sitting across from her with the guy who'd been sprawled on the bedroom floor last night, pale and sweating in pain.

"It belongs to my brother, but I'd be happy to take you both out for a ride if you're interested."

Derek grinned with excitement. He cocked his head and glanced down at his daughter. "What do you think, Lexi? Do you want to go for a boat ride?"

Lexi's expression lit up. "Yes!" It was the most enthusiasm she'd seen from the girl since bringing them both home last night.

"Well then, sounds like a plan," Julie said, betraying her eagerness. She finished her slice of pizza and pushed away from the table. "You'll have to give me a few minutes to make sure everything is clean. I haven't had the boat out in two weeks."

"Sit down and finish your lunch, Julie," Derek said

firmly. "There's no rush. Lexi and I can help clean up the boat if needed."

The fact that he was supposed to be resting seemed to be lost on him, but she bit back her argument and sank back down, helping herself to another small slice of pizza. She gave up trying to lecture him, since it didn't do any good anyway.

After they finished the entire pizza, Derek making a much bigger dent than he had last night, she tossed the empty box in the garbage and then went back inside to fill a pail with warm, soapy water.

Derek and Lexi were waiting patiently for her out on the patio, and, of course, Derek took the pail of water from her before they walked down to the lake together. If his ribs were aching, he made sure the pain didn't show on his face.

She removed the boat cover, grimacing when she saw that the seats were lightly coated with dirt. But with all three of them working together, it didn't take long before the boat was sparkling clean.

She hauled out Amelia's life vest for Lexi and instructed the girl on how to put it on. Lexi didn't seem thrilled but, after a stern look from her father, didn't complain. Julie slid the key into the ignition and glanced over at Derek and Lexi. "Are you ready?"

Derek nodded. "Sure."

Knowing that bouncing over the waves might cause him pain, she started out at a slow pace. The lake was busy, so she had to carefully navigate the craft around the other boaters, making sure to keep an eye out for skiers and tubers. When she came upon an open stretch of lake, she pushed the throttle forward, kicking up some speed, and was rewarded by Lexi's laughter.

All too soon, she had to slow back down, carefully

turning around to head back toward her home. She glanced over at her passengers, glad to see Derek looked relaxed, with Lexi tucked close to his side.

"I don't suppose you'd let me drive?" he asked, capturing her gaze with his.

"Sure, why not?" she pulled the throttle back so that the boat was idling as they awkwardly switched seats. His arm brushed hers, and she had no business inhaling his masculine scent, especially since it went straight to her head. She moved away, taking a seat across from Lexi.

As Derek drove them leisurely around the lake, she could feel the curious stares from some of her friends and neighbors. The smile on her features dimmed as she realized what this little outing probably looked like to everyone else. As if she and Derek were seeing each other on a personal level.

She closed her eyes for a moment, dreading the thought of being the source of more rumors. The gossip had flown fast and furious after Andrew had left her. Being out in public like this would only encourage the small town tongues to start flapping all over again.

Leaving her to explain why Derek and Lexi had left, as she knew they would, right after the holiday.

———

DEREK ENJOYED BEING out on the boat, but as soon as he realized the three of them were becoming the center of attention, he turned the boat around to head back to Julie's place.

Stupid to forget, even for a moment, that he and Lexi needed to keep a low profile. As far as he knew, Julie hadn't so much as turned on a radio or a television since last night, but that didn't mean her neighbors hadn't. He'd already pushed his luck with Deputy Thomas.

Lexi was legally in his custody, but that didn't mean Claire's parents weren't still searching for them. And who knows what story they might have told the police?

After all, they had wealth and power on their side when all he had was love.

"Let's go again, Daddy," Lexi said with a rare pout.

"Sorry, baby-doll, but my ribs are still a little sore," he said. He wasn't lying, because his ribs did ache—not that he'd let a little pain get in the way of making Lexi happy.

Going to the private school that Claire's parents had forced upon her hadn't made her happy, either. Keeping her safe was more important. And the fear of being found by Claire's parents trumped another boat ride by far.

"We can go out again another day," Julie assured Lexi. "Maybe even tomorrow afternoon. I have to go to church in the morning and then stop at the grocery store, but then we have the rest of the day free."

He wasn't surprised that Julie planned to go to church since she'd mentioned that to the doc, but the flash of guilt caught him off guard. He ignored the emotion as he carefully pulled the speedboat into its docking station next to the pier. "Lexi, why don't you get your sketchbook? I bet Julie would appreciate a pretty picture of her lake."

"Oh, I'd love that," Julie agreed with enthusiasm. "Would you do that for me, Lexi? Please?"

His daughter gave another of her reserved, tiny nods, and he was relieved she'd allowed herself to be distracted from taking another trip around the lake. He shut off the motor and helped Lexi out of the boat first, before reaching down to help Julie with the cover.

"I'll get it. You need to rest those ribs," she said.

"I'm not an invalid," he muttered, his tone sharper than he intended. He knew she was reacting to the excuse he'd given to Lexi for going back home, which made him feel guilty again. Hadn't Julie noticed the way people stared at them?

"I know, but I can do this," she said. "Why don't you take Lexi back up to the house?"

Julie was avoiding his gaze, and he realized maybe she had noticed the curious stares and was embarrassed to be seen with him and Lexi. The thought bothered him, even though he knew Julie's personal life was none of his business.

For all he knew, she might be seeing someone, although she certainly hadn't mentioned it. He almost asked her but then gave himself a mental shake. "All right, let's go, Lexi."

He climbed off the boat and took his daughter's hand. Lexi seemed to hesitate, but after one last glance over her shoulder at Julie, she came along with him.

He didn't relax until they were back up at the patio outside the townhouse, away from the curious eyes of Julie's neighbors. He gingerly lowered himself into one of the patio chairs while Lexi ran inside the townhouse for her sketchbook.

His ribs were still sore, but the ache in his head seemed to be a bit better. Being out on the lake had been wonderful; for a few brief moments, it had been nice to forget all his worries and enjoy being out on the water. But then reality had crashed through his false sense of security.

He wasn't here to have fun. He needed to figure out where he could find a job and a place to live. Someplace where he could establish himself in a community, making it difficult for Claire's parents to take Lexi away from him. If that was even possible.

He closed his eyes for a moment, rubbing a hand along the right side of his chest. There was nothing worse than feeling useless. He wished he felt strong enough to start working on the half-gutted townhouse. The sooner he could pay Julie back for her hospitality, the better.

Lexi came back outside and climbed into the seat beside him. He opened his eyes, blinking against the bright sunlight. Thankfully, the umbrella overhead helped provide some shade, and he watched as Lexi pulled out her colored pencils and began to draw the lake.

"Would you like some iced tea or a soft drink?" Julie asked as she walked up.

"Sure. Tea would be great," he said, even though he knew that he was already imposing on Julie far more than he had a right to.

"Lexi, do you like root beer?" Julie asked.

His daughter nodded but didn't look up from her drawing. Once his daughter was preoccupied with something she liked to do, it was difficult to get her attention. He was about to apologize for Lexi's behavior, but Julie was already disappearing into her side of the townhouse, the screen door sliding shut behind her.

He allowed his eyes to drift closed, giving in to a wave of insidious fatigue. Why he should be so tired, he had no idea. It wasn't as if he'd done much. And if he was this exhausted just from running a few errands and going for a boat ride, then how in the world was he going to do the construction work on Julie's townhouse that needed to be done?

"Derek, why don't you go inside to lie down?"

He pried his eyes open and summoned a smile. "It's nice

being out here like this." He reached for the glass of ice-cold tea. "Thanks, again."

Julie gave him an exasperated look as she sat down beside him. "I don't know what you're trying to prove," she muttered. "It hasn't even been twenty-four hours since your accident."

He didn't want to think about the crash. "Does your brother live around here?"

"He lives about an hour away in Madison," she said. "Unfortunately, Zack doesn't get up here as much as he used to. Still, we've stayed close since our parents died."

There was a hint of sadness in her tone, but he held back from asking anything too personal. After all, it wasn't as if he wanted to reciprocate. Julie seemed like the type of woman who'd feel compelled to report him to the authorities if she knew the truth.

"This area looks like a nice place to live," he said instead. "How many people are there in Crystal Lake?"

"About fourteen hundred people live within Hope County, and over half of them live within a twenty-five mile radius to the lake. The people here either work at the medical center, for the government either in city hall or the sheriff's department, or in the service sector, which depends a lot on tourism to survive."

"No manufacturing jobs, huh?" he asked.

"No. We had a car manufacturing plant about thirty miles from here, but that closed down a few years ago, after the collapse of the economy."

He figured as much. Crystal Lake might be a great place to live, but he needed some sort of job that would support him and Lexi. He'd done some construction work prior to going into the service, but with the economy the way it was, no one was building new houses anymore.

Eight years in the Army hadn't exactly prepared him for the civilian job market. Of course, he'd planned to reenlist until Claire had told him about her cancer. The doctor had given her six months to live.

She'd only lasted four.

Seven years ago, when Claire had discovered she was pregnant, he'd asked her to marry him, but she'd refused. At least Claire had let him be a part of Lexi's life, and not only had he sent most of his money to Claire, he'd spent as much time as he could with Lexi. But after Claire had found out about her cancer, she'd asked him to come back to care for their daughter. He'd jumped through yards of red tape before he was granted his honorary discharge, but it was several weeks too late. Claire had passed away, and Lexi had ended up living with Claire's parents until he'd arrived stateside. Thankfully, Lexi hadn't forgotten him and had clung to his shoulders like a little monkey, as if she'd never let him go.

It had been his first inkling of what the child had gone through with her grandparents. Apparently, even when Claire was too weak to care for Lexi, her parents had taken over, enrolling her in that ridiculous private school where she was punished if she didn't act like the other kids.

Which had been most of the time.

He still saw red when he thought about what Lexi had been through, so he forced the images away. He was not about to let Claire's parents get custody of Lexi. In the few weeks they'd been together, Lexi had already begun to relax and trust him. Now more than ever, he believed he'd made the right decision to take her away. He and Lexi would make things work.

"Here, Julie, this is for you." His daughter's voice pulled

him away from his thoughts. He was surprised that Lexi had opened up even that much to a virtual stranger.

"Lexi, this is a beautiful picture," Julie said with awe. "The detail is absolutely amazing. I had no idea you were so talented."

Glancing over, he caught the shy smile his daughter flashed at Julie. The hero worship was clear in Lexi's bright blue eyes.

In that moment, the truth sucker punched him, stealing his breath.

Lexi was looking up to Julie like a surrogate mother.

And when it was time for them to leave, his daughter would be hurt all over again.

6

J ulie was truly stunned at how talented Lexi was and couldn't help staring at the lake drawing, marveling at the detail. She'd loved Amelia with all her heart, but her niece's pictures had been stick people and crude landmarks. Nothing like Lexi's precise drawing of the lake within which everything was amazingly to scale.

As silence hung heavily, she scrambled for something to talk about. "I thought we'd have burgers for dinner if that's okay with you," she offered, glancing over at Derek.

"Sounds good," he agreed.

She stared at him for a moment, feeling as if there might be something wrong, and not just because he was avoiding her gaze. The silence stretched between them, only not as relaxing as it had been earlier.

As the sun began its slow descent on the horizon, she took Lexi's drawing with her and went into the kitchen to begin making the hamburger patties. Through the window, she noticed Derek slowly rise to his feet and walk over to the grill.

She took the plate of raw burgers outside, and Derek

barely glanced at her as he took the plate. "I'll make them," he said.

"Thanks." She returned to the kitchen for the salad, wondering why there was this weird tension between them. Had she said something wrong? Or was he simply tired from being outside all day?

She took the salad bowl out and set it on the patio table. "Lexi, would you mind helping me bring out the plates, napkins, silverware, and condiments?"

Lexi nodded and readily slid down off the chair. Derek glanced over, and she hesitated, getting the impression that he was about to say something. But then he simply turned back to the grill, using the spatula to flip the burgers.

The rest of the meal was just as strained, despite her efforts to chat. It seemed that the easy camaraderie that had existed between them had disappeared without a trace. And she had no idea why. When the meal was over, Derek and Lexi helped her carry everything back inside but then disappeared into their side of the townhouse.

As she washed the dishes, she wondered if Derek's ribs were hurting him more than he'd let on. Certainly, she understood if he needed rest. But why did it seem that there was something more bothering him?

When she finished with dinner, she went back outside to sit on one of her patio chairs to watch the sun set over the lake, feeling a strange sense of loneliness without Derek and Lexi seated beside her.

THE NEXT MORNING, Julie ate a bowl of cold cereal before

getting dressed for church. She chose a flowery skirt and a matching blouse and then took the time to blow-dry her hair so that it was nice and straight. She headed over to the adjacent townhouse and knocked on the screen door. After a few minutes with no response, she called out, "Derek? Lexi?"

A dark shadow appeared, and she noticed with relief that Derek was standing on the other side of the screen.

"Good morning," Derek said quietly. His hair was damp from a recent shower, and he was dressed in a clean pair of jeans and a red T-shirt, an acute reminder that he had regular clothes rather than the scrubs. He appeared more rested than he had the day before, and she suspected that no one seeing him like this would believe he'd suffered a collapsed lung and bruised ribs less than forty-eight hours ago. Obviously, he was a quick healer.

"Good morning." She smoothed a hand over her skirt, feeling nervous. "Um...I have cold cereal for breakfast if you and Lexi are hungry. And I was wondering if you and Lexi wanted to attend church services with me this morning?"

"Cereal sounds fine, but I think we'll pass on the church services," he murmured. "Thanks anyway."

She did her best to keep the keen sense of disappointment from her features, even though she knew that if Derek and Lexi had come with her, the town gossips would have had a field day. Certainly it was better this way.

So why was she so upset?

"All right, I'll be heading out shortly, but please help yourself to whatever you need in the kitchen, okay?" She pasted a bright smile on her face with an effort. "I'll see you both later." Fighting tears, she turned away.

"Julie," he said in a low voice.

She stopped and took a deep breath before turning back to face him. "Yes?"

"Thank you, for everything."

Her mouth went dry, and for a wild moment, she thought he was saying goodbye. But how could Derek and Lexi possibly leave? As far as she knew, there weren't many places nearby to rent a car, especially on a Sunday.

"You're welcome," she managed. As she turned and walked back to her side of the townhouse, she paused in the kitchen, gripping the back of a kitchen chair, inwardly debating the idea of forgoing church services. Maybe if she stayed here, Derek and Lexi wouldn't leave. She'd find a way to convince them to stay, at least through the holiday.

But as soon as the thought crossed her mind, she knew she was being ridiculous. She still needed to go grocery shopping, or they'd all starve. And whether she liked it or not, Derek and Lexi had every right to leave her townhouse and Crystal Lake whenever they wanted to.

Her fault if she found that idea depressing.

Maybe praying would help her find peace. She straightened her shoulders and grabbed her purse and car keys before heading for the door. She would go to church, and she would go grocery shopping afterwards. And if Derek and Lexi were gone when she returned, then obviously, that was God's will.

If she could survive the scandal of Andrew's affair, she'd certainly survive Derek and Lexi leaving.

Better for her to remember her role here was simply to help a stranger and his daughter in need. Derek wasn't looking for anything more.

And she shouldn't be, either.

––––––––––

DEREK LEANED on the door frame, fighting the urge to call
Julie back. The flash of disappointment in her eyes had cut
deep, even though he knew he couldn't afford to be seen
with Lexi in such a public place. For all he knew, Deputy
Thomas would be there, or some of the other members of
the town's law enforcement. If Claire's parents had
sounded the alarm they may recognize him and
arrest him.

He hadn't been to church in years, but surprisingly, he
realized he'd have liked to go with Julie.

Lexi came up to stand beside him, and he forced himself
to focus on his daughter. "Are you hungry, baby-doll?" he
asked in a lighthearted tone.

"Yes," she said with a shy smile.

"All right, give me a few minutes to clean up first, and
we'll find something to eat, okay?"

As he finished making their beds, he heard the sound of
Julie's car driving away and winced at the flash of guilt. Julie
had been nothing but kind to them, and he felt bad at the
way he'd acted last night, putting distance between them.

But at the same time, he couldn't afford to cause his
daughter any more pain.

Time to get himself back on track. He walked back into
the main living area to find Lexi waiting impatiently. "Let's
get some cereal, okay?"

She followed him next door, and he couldn't deny
feeling like an intruder as he rummaged through Julie's
kitchen. With Lexi's help, he found the box of cereal, bowls,
spoons, and milk.

They ate at the kitchen table, overlooking the lake,
which was surprisingly noisy with boaters and skiers

making the most out of another glorious day. Apparently the tourists didn't bother attending church services either.

Lexi looked longingly out toward the water, and he knew she wanted to swim. He needed to get some work done on the townhouse as a way to repay Julie's kindness, but he didn't want to disappoint his daughter, either. Although he needed to get rid of the stupid catheter in his chest, too. If Dr. Allen didn't show up, he figured he could pull it out himself, no problem.

"I have to do some work first, Lexi, but when I'm finished, we can go down and swim, okay?"

She scowled and kicked her feet rhythmically under the table. He recognized the signs of her distress, but as much as he cherished his relationship with Lexi, she also needed to learn that she couldn't always have her way.

"Work first, then play," he repeated. He stood and took the bowls to the sink. Julie had left hers there as well, so he filled the sink with soapy water, washed and dried them before putting everything back where he'd found them. Lexi had stubbornly remained at the kitchen table, swinging her legs and rocking a bit, but he didn't say anything. Bringing attention to her behavior never helped. Something he'd tried to explain to Claire's parents, to no avail.

"I'll be right next door if you need something," he said, pretending he wasn't bothered by his daughter's silent motion as he slipped outside.

Back inside the gutted portion of the townhouse, he picked up the crowbar and began pulling down the remainder of the blackened drywall. Within ten minutes, he was covered with dust and sweat, but despite the throbbing pain across his ribs, he felt a keen satisfaction at his slow but methodical progress.

The patio doors opened, and Lexi came inside, and the

tension around his chest eased a bit. It was one thing to tell himself that it was best to leave Lexi alone when she got in one of her moods, but following his own advice was far from easy.

"Hey, baby-doll, stay back so you don't get hurt, okay?"

She gave a small nod and stayed near the patio doors as he continued to rip down the drywall. When Lexi put her hands over her ears in response to the noise, he stopped with a sigh.

He swiped the hem of his T-shirt across his forehead and set the crowbar aside. He crossed over to Lexi. "Why don't you sit outside on the patio for a bit?" he suggested. "I should be done here in about an hour, and then we can swim, okay?"

She stared at him for a long moment, dark reproach in her blue eyes, but he steeled his heart against giving in.

"Lexi, Julie has helped us a lot, hasn't she?" he asked.

His daughter's lips formed a pout, but she nodded her agreement.

"I'm doing this to help Julie. She's giving us food and a place to sleep. All I'm asking is for an hour or so to do some work for her." He didn't bother explaining that his sore ribs wouldn't tolerate much longer than that anyway. "Don't you think that's the right thing to do?"

Lexi scowled but gave another nod.

"Good girl," he said. "What would you rather do? Sit and read in your room? Play video games? Or sit outside and draw?"

"Draw," Lexi said promptly, and he grinned again, wondering why he'd bothered to ask. Lexi could easily spend hours drawing, which had been another problem with that private school Claire's parents had enrolled her in. The teachers there were all about learning, which was fine, but they didn't provide any time for Lexi's drawing. And they forced her to interact with the other kids, which Lexi found very distressing. And when she didn't socialize with the other kids or raise her hand in class, the teacher made her sit outside in the hall. The memory made his blood boil.

He forced the memories aside. "Okay. Let's get your sketchbook, okay?" He went over to find her book and her pencils and carried them outside. He glanced at the lake and then turned back to Lexi. "No swimming without me, all right?"

"I know," she said, barely casting him a glance as she reached for her pencil.

He sat down beside her, catching her gaze with his. "I mean it, Lexi. No swimming without me."

She must have recognized the seriousness of his tone, because she said, "I know, Daddy."

"Good." He stood and made his way back inside to finish pulling down the drywall. As he worked, he kept an eye on his daughter. But he needn't have worried. When Lexi concentrated on drawing, the rest of the world ceased to exist.

And for once he was glad for his daughter's single-minded focus.

———

JULIE TRIED to pay attention to the church services, but once the final hymn had been sung and she'd followed her fellow parishioners outside, she couldn't remember what the theme of the pastor's sermon had been.

She smiled and greeted people as she made her way to

her car, too preoccupied to notice that a few of them were looking at her with frank curiosity. No doubt, the rumors were already flying about how she'd been seen with the tall, dark stranger and his daughter.

The next stop was the grocery store, and she mentally reviewed her list as she pushed her cart up and down the rows, moving fast. Too fast, because then she forgot something and had to go back for it. It wasn't until she was in line at the register, tapping her foot impatiently, that she realized her stomach was knotted with anxiety.

A sensation that didn't ease as she transferred her groceries into the trunk of her car. After sliding behind the wheel, she had to remind herself not to speed through town as she headed home.

As she pulled into her driveway, she glanced around for any sign of Derek or Lexi. But even though the windows were open, she didn't hear a sound from their side of the townhouse.

Her heart lodged in her throat as she opened the trunk and walked around to pick up one bag of groceries. She practically raced inside and set the bag down on the kitchen table before crossing over to the patio doors.

The sound of Lexi's laughter stopped her, and she let out a sigh of relief when she saw two heads bobbing in the water near shore, evidence that Derek and Lexi were swimming in the lake.

They were still here.

Derek hadn't been telling her goodbye after all.

Every bit of apprehension that she'd felt since she left earlier that morning faded away as she watched father and daughter playing in the water.

Suddenly, she abruptly straightened. What in the world

was Derek thinking? He shouldn't be swimming! Not when he still had the catheter in his chest.

In a flash, she threw open the patio doors and ran down the grassy slope to the lakeshore. "Derek! Get out of the water! That catheter site is going to get infected!"

Derek stood and carried Lexi over to the shore. After he set his daughter on her feet, he swiped his wet hair from his face. "Calm down. Your friendly doctor Gabe Allen stopped by with his fiancée Larissa and took the catheter out."

She vaguely remembered Gabe offering to do that when they were in the hospital yesterday. She shouldn't have been surprised, Gabe was a great guy and this is exactly something he'd do. How had she missed seeing Gabe and Larissa at church? "Really?"

"Yes, and he gave me some water-proof dressings to put over the small incision while swimming. So you see? There's nothing to worry about."

She scowled and planted her hands on her hips. "I highly doubt he meant for you to swim in the lake. Those dressings are for showering with clean water."

"I promise, he really did say I could swim in the lake," Derek insisted.

"Okay, okay." Was she overreacting? Maybe. "If you don't mind, I'll take a look at the wound after lunch. Just in case." She turned and walked back up to the house, belatedly realizing that she'd left the rest of the groceries in the car. Never before had a man sent her from exasperated to happy within five minutes. Andrew had mostly made her sad. She shrugged and brought in another bag of groceries.

"Would you like some help?" Derek asked once he'd dried himself off with a towel.

"I'm fine," she said, knowing that Derek would only get in the way since he didn't know where everything went anyway. "I bought cold cuts and Italian bread to make sand-wiches for lunch."

"Sounds good." Derek stood near the door, and the minute she'd emptied the last grocery bag, he took her hand. "Come on, I want to show you something."

Far too conscious of his hand wrapped around hers, she curiously followed him outside to the set of patio doors leading into the other side of the townhouse. And when she walked in, she gasped in surprise. All of the drywall had been taken down off the walls of the living room and kitchen area, while the floor had been swept clean.

"You did all this today?" she asked in awe.

He nodded. "I still need to do the ceiling, but taking old drywall down is a lot easier than putting new stuff up. Although I should be able to get to that in a couple of days."

"I...don't know what to say," she murmured, her cheeks pink with gratitude. All this time, she'd feared that Derek and Lexi were leaving, when in fact, he'd been working as a show of good faith in keeping up his end of the bargain.

And in that moment, she grimly realized that, despite her best efforts, she'd grown far too emotionally attached to Derek and Lexi.

A path that would surely lead to heartbreak.

7

As Julie fixed lunch, she couldn't help noticing how Derek was moving slowly and carefully again as he crossed the patio and sat down at the table. No doubt the physical work he'd done earlier, tearing down most of her old drywall, had been too much.

Granted, she very much appreciated the work he'd done, but at the same time, she didn't want him to hurt himself again, either.

She brought out the sandwiches and chips she'd picked up at the store and then went back inside for soft drinks. She chose iced tea for herself and Derek, and a tall glass of ice-cold milk for Lexi.

Both Derek and Lexi sat with their hands together, as if waiting for her to pray. Once she'd taken her seat, she bowed her head and took a deep breath, letting it out slowly. "Dear Lord, we thank You for the food You've provided for us today, and we ask for Your wisdom in guiding us on the path You want us to take, especially Derek, who seems intent on working too hard when he's still in pain. We ask this in the name of Christ the Lord. Amen."

She heard a choked laugh as she opened her eyes to find Derek fighting a smile. She pinned him with a stern look. "I'm not kidding," she muttered. "You need to listen to what your body is telling you."

"I know, but I'm fine."

"Yeah, I've heard that before," she said wryly. "You always say that, no matter how much pain you're in. And don't think I've forgotten about your dressing, because I haven't. As soon as we're finished here, I'm going to take a look at your catheter site."

"Yes, Nurse Julie," he responded lightly.

She smiled in spite of herself and glanced at Lexi, who was eating her sandwich with gusto. Julie was glad Lexi didn't seem to be a picky eater, the way Amelia had been. Finding foods that Amelia would eat, even before she'd started chemotherapy, had been a challenge. When the chemo had started, Amelia had lost several pounds, until the child was nothing but skin and bones.

"Julie, why are you sad?" Lexi asked.

She pulled her mind away from the painful memories. "I was thinking about my niece, Amelia," she said honestly. "Sometimes you remind me of her."

Lexi's blue eyes, mirror images of her father's, regarded her steadily. "And that makes you sad?"

"More happy than sad," she corrected. "So tell me how you enjoyed swimming in the lake. Did the seaweed bother you?"

Lexi wrinkled her nose. "A little, but my daddy held me up and kept me away from the weeds."

"That's great, Lexi," Julie said with a smile. "And I'm sure you'll get used to the seaweed."

Derek raised a brow, and she belatedly realized she'd done it again, assuming they'd be staying longer than a few days. What in the world was wrong with her? She needed to think of Derek as a patient, not as a single father. Or a handsome man.

As soon as they were finished with lunch, she jumped up and began carrying things inside. Derek and Lexi helped, so it didn't take long to put everything away. When they were finished, Lexi went back outside to her drawing. She stopped Derek from following his daughter, gesturing to the kitchen table.

"Sit down," she said to Derek in her best don't-mess-with-me tone. "I want to clean that wound."

He looked as if he might argue but then gingerly lowered himself onto one of the kitchen chairs as she went into the bathroom to get her first aid kit. When she returned, she noticed Derek was watching his daughter, who was engrossed in her drawing.

"She's quite the artist," she murmured as she opened the kit and set out the supplies.

"I know, and she can draw for hours if I let her," Derek agreed.

She filled a bowl with hot water and then brought over the bowl, a clean washcloth, and some mild soap. "At least it's better than playing video games."

"Trust me, she does that, too." Derek slid his arm out of his T-shirt and held his elbow up so she could look at the small puncture site.

"This might hurt a bit," she warned as she peeled the clear, transparent, waterproof dressing off. She was surprised to see that the skin beneath was nice and dry. The puncture site was small and seemed relatively clean.

"How bad does it look?" Derek asked.

"Not as bad as I expected," she grudgingly admitted. She did her best to focus her attention on the task at hand and not the masculine scent of Derek's skin. After dipping the washcloth in the hot water, she gently cleaned the wound. When she glanced up at Derek, she was disconcerted to find his face was mere inches from hers.

She stared into his eyes for a long moment before taking a step back. She glanced around for the antibiotic ointment, a bit flustered by his nearness. "I'll, um, just use a bit of this and cover it with gauze for now," she said, knowing she was babbling but unable to make herself stop. "We'll save those waterproof dressings for swimming and showering, okay?"

"Sounds good," he murmured.

Stop talking, she told herself as she taped the two-by-two square gauze over the small puncture site. She straightened, trying to hide shaking fingers. "All finished," she said in a breathless tone.

"Thanks, Julie," he said as he put his arm back through the sleeve of his T-shirt.

She gave a terse nod and leaned forward to gather up her supplies at the same instant Derek chose to stand, the movement causing them to bump into each other.

When Derek's hands lightly grasped her waist to steady her, her breath lodged in her throat, and her heart rate kicked into triple digits.

Overwhelmed by his nearness, she looked up at him at the same time he tipped his head down toward hers. His blue eyes were dark and intent, and when he lowered his mouth to hers, she didn't move. Didn't blink.

There was nothing she wanted more than Derek's kiss.

His mouth settled over hers, and she gently parted her lips, reveling in his taste, leaning against him when her knees went weak.

"Daddy?" Lexi's voice crashed the moment.

Derek pulled away so quickly she lost her balance and

had to grab on to the kitchen table for support as Derek hastened to put distance between them. "What's up, baby-doll?" he asked in a hoarse tone. She couldn't help being glad that he'd obviously been as affected as she was by their kiss.

"Do you want to see my drawing?" Lexi asked.

"Of course I do," he said, moving forward to escape through the patio doors. The spring door slid shut with a bang behind him.

Julie stayed where she was for several long moments, trying to rein in her rioting emotions.

Why had he kissed her? Why had she kissed him back? Well, she knew why she'd kissed him back, because really, what sane woman wouldn't? Derek was tall, dark and handsome, not to mention gentle and kind.

But she truly had no idea why he'd kissed her in the first place. Andrew had found her attractive at first but then had lost patience with her. He'd ended up getting back together with his old girlfriend. She'd be better off staying far away from Derek. But as she cleaned up the first aid supplies and dumped out the water in the sink, she couldn't stop wondering if or when Derek might kiss her again.

———————

DEREK MENTALLY BERATED himself for being an idiot as he peered down at Lexi's drawing. Why had he kissed Julie like that? She was a beautiful, kind, Christian woman who had gone out of her way to help him and Lexi. And how had he thanked her? By giving in to the need to kiss her.

He'd be lucky if she didn't immediately demand they leave, after the stunt he'd pulled.

He forced himself to concentrate on Lexi's drawing. She'd chosen to do a picture of Julie's townhouse this time, rather than the lake, and he had to admit, his daughter had an eye for detail. She'd even included Julie's small vegetable garden.

"It's beautiful, Lexi," he said honestly. "Just like you."

"Will Julie like it?"

"Of course she will." He shouldn't have been surprised by Lexi's desire to make Julie happy, but he was. Since they'd left St. Louis, Lexi hadn't said a word about her mother's death or her grandparents. It was as if his daughter had pushed away all the bad memories of the past. He only hoped they wouldn't come out to haunt her when she least expected it.

"I'll give to Julie," Lexi said, picking up the drawing and heading toward the patio doors. When Lexi disappeared inside, he scrubbed his hands over his face.

Lexi hadn't mentioned seeing the two of them kissing, but then again, Lexi didn't have much use for conversation in general. He sincerely hoped his daughter hadn't noticed. The last thing he wanted to do was to hurt Lexi in any way. He took a deep breath and winced when his ribs protested.

The very idea that Julie might ask them to leave made him feel like a jerk. And for the first time in years, he offered up a silent prayer. *Please, Lord, give me the strength to do what is right for Julie and for Lexi.*

Surprisingly, he felt calmer after the prayer. Was it possible God was still listening to him? A soldier who'd sinned more times than he could count? Once, he'd believed in God's willingness to forgive, but he wasn't so sure that killing Afghani soldiers was something that God would condone. Not to mention the fact that he and Claire had created Lexi outside of the sanctity of marriage. So many sins. Too many sins.

But he could believe that Julie had God's protection, so maybe, just maybe, his prayer wouldn't fall on deaf ears.

Somehow, he had to find a way to keep his guard up around Julie. They could be friends, but nothing more. He headed toward the townhouse he was sharing with Lexi and picked up the crowbar again.

The best thing he could do for Julie was to repay her kindness—not by kissing the living daylights out of her, but by helping to finish up her construction project. So he climbed the small stepladder and ignored the stab of pain rippling across his chest as he began chipping away at the old drywall on the ceiling.

Julie deserved better than a jobless man on the run with his daughter, and the sooner he remembered that fact, the better.

———

DEREK WORKED on the task of bringing down the rest of the drywall covering the ceiling until he was in so much pain he couldn't lift his arms anymore. He climbed down from the stepladder and propped the crowbar against one of the two-by-four studs, pressing a hand to his aching ribs. Assailed by a sudden wave of dizziness, he sank down to the floor and concentrated on not passing out cold.

He closed his eyes and tipped his head back against the two-by-four studs, taking one slow breath followed by another, willing the dizziness to recede. He knew very well he needed to pull himself together before Julie happened to show up to find him like this. She'd be disappointed again, maybe even angry enough to yell at him, rightfully so, although in a way, this was all her fault.

The hard work and subsequent pain had pushed thoughts of kissing her again right out of his mind.

A reluctant smile tugged at the corner of his mouth. Okay, maybe it was best not to mention that fact if she came looking for him.

After a few minutes, the room stopped spinning, and he opened his eyes, longing for a drink of ice-cold water or the sun tea Julie loved. But getting something to drink would require him to move, so he decided to stay right where he was for a little longer.

The throbbing of his ribs didn't ease much, telling him he'd overdone it big-time. But as he stared up at the ceiling, he was satisfied to realize he'd managed to get more than a quarter of the ceiling drywall down. Not too bad for a man who'd been in a car crash recently.

He estimated that he would have the rest of the drywall down by the Fourth of July, which would be perfect timing. He didn't dare stay in Hope County too long, even though it felt good to be doing something constructive rather than driving aimlessly, looking for a place that might be hiring.

He stared at the half-demolished kitchen and living room area and considered staying long enough to get the entire job finished. But as soon as the thought formed, he dismissed it.

For one thing, Julie might not have the money to purchase the necessary supplies. Drywall, cabinets, counters, and sinks had a way of adding up to a pretty penny. There were about five sheets of drywall propped in one corner, but that wouldn't be nearly enough to finish the open-concept room.

No, best that he complete as much of the work as possible before hitting the road with Lexi.

"Derek?"

Julie's voice came from outside, not from the patio but from the front yard.

"Coming," he called, forcing himself to move. Getting back on his feet was no easy task, and by the time he managed the feat, tiny beads of sweat were rolling down his temples.

For a long moment, he stood bracing himself against the wall, trying to gather the strength he'd need to face Julie without letting on how much pain he was in. She'd take it personally even though it was his own stupid fault for over-exerting himself.

"Derek? Come on, I want you to meet my brother, Zack," Julie called again, a note of impatience lacing her tone.

"I'm coming," he assured her. He used the hem of his T-shirt to swipe away the sweat and stepped carefully over the drywall debris littering the floor as he made his way across the room. He pasted a broad smile on his face in an attempt to hide his discomfort as he opened the front door.

"There you are," Julie exclaimed. She stood next to a tall man with medium-brown hair. "Derek, this is my brother, Zack Crain. Zack, this is Derek Ryerson, Lexi's father."

His greeting died in his throat when he stared in horror at the police car parked at the end of Julie's driveway. It took another second or two for his brain to register that Zack was dressed in uniform blue, complete with a shiny badge pinned to his chest and a gun nestled at his waist.

Why on earth hadn't Julie mentioned her brother was a cop?

8

D erek forced himself to approach Julie and her brother, ignoring the tight knot of anxiety twisting his gut. "Nice to meet you, Zack," he said, reluctantly holding out his hand. "Sorry about the dust and sweat."

Zack's gaze narrowed a bit, but he returned the greeting. "No problem. Good to meet you, too." The handshake was hard and brief.

Derek let his hand drop to his side and wondered how long it would take for Julie's brother to run a background check on him. Probably not long. Would he even wait to leave or run the check right now in his squad car?

His pulse jumped erratically, and he knew he should take Lexi and leave right away. But how? A rental car? Maybe he could afford a rental, at least until he got to a bus station. And then what?

Where would he go? What would he and Lexi do?

"Derek, are you all right?" Julie asked, pulling him from his panicked thoughts.

"Um, yeah. Sorry. What did you say?"

"I was telling Zack about the work you've been doing on the townhouse," she said. A hint of concern shadowed her eyes.

"Right. Actually, I just pulled more drywall off the ceiling, and it's a bit of a mess. Why don't you wait here while I clean things up?" He couldn't deny he was desperate to get away. Maybe he could convince Julie's brother that he was harmless. And then maybe, just maybe, her brother the cop wouldn't run a background check only to find Claire's parents had filed for custody.

But the shred of hope wasn't reassuring. Not when he knew that, if the situation were reversed, he'd be doing a background check on a stranger who was sharing a townhouse with his sister.

He turned and walked back inside, letting the screen door slam shut behind him, trying to act natural as he began sweeping up the debris littering the floor. When Julie, Zack, and Lexi came inside, he stopped and leaned on the broom, trying to look casual when in fact he feared his legs might buckle beneath him. "What do you think?" he asked, striving for a normal tone.

"Wow, looks great," Julie said in awe. Then she frowned. "Your ribs must be killing you. It can't be easy working on the ceiling."

He shrugged. "The results are worth it."

Zack stared at him, his gaze faintly accusatory. "How long are you planning to stay?"

"Until after the holiday," Derek murmured. "Hopefully by then, my car will be replaced and I'll be able to hit the road again."

"What? No. Knock it off, Zack," Julie said in a stern tone. "I'm thrilled to have Derek and Lexi here. And I told you, we have a mutually beneficial arrangement. He and Lexi get food and a roof over their heads, and in return, I get work done on the townhouse. It's a win-win for both of us."

"Yeah, that's what I'm afraid of," Zack muttered darkly.

Derek tried to control a flash of anger on Julie's behalf. "I don't like what you're insinuating," he said in a clipped tone. "Julie has been nothing but kind. Lexi and I are very grateful for her willingness to give us food and shelter. It's not my intent to take advantage of your sister. She's perfectly safe."

Lexi must have noticed some of the tension in the room because she came over to stand close to his side. He put a reassuring arm around his daughter, hugging her close.

Surprisingly, a spasm of pain flashed across Zack's features, and he rather abruptly turned away.

"Are you planning to stay for dinner, Zack?" Julie asked in an obvious effort to change the subject.

"No, I have to get back. Thanks anyway." Zack walked back outside and settled his police hat back on his head.

Derek's shoulders slumped with relief at the news her brother wasn't planning on staying, but that didn't change the fact that he needed to figure out a way to get out of town. And soon.

Before his luck ran out.

———

JULIE FOLLOWED her brother back to his squad car. "Zack, please consider staying for dinner," she murmured. "Derek is really a nice guy."

Zack shook his head, avoiding her gaze. "I can't. The way he looks with his daughter..." He sighed and scrubbed his hands over his face. "I just can't."

She knew how difficult losing Amelia had been for Zack. No parent should have to lose both his spouse and his daughter within a two-year timeframe. She wanted to help ease his pain, tried to convince him to hand his burdens over to God, but Zack refused.

Her brother hadn't stepped foot in a church since losing Emma and Amelia. Her heart ached for him. They'd grown closer over the years since losing their parents.

"Goodbye, Julie," Zack said as he slid into the driver's seat.

She forced a smile. "Bye, Zack. Stop by again soon."

He gave a terse nod as he twisted the key, bringing the engine to life. But he didn't back out of the driveway right away. Instead, he lowered the passenger window. "Are you sure you can trust this guy?"

"Absolutely," she said, as if she hadn't had the exact same fears just yesterday. But that was before the kiss. Interesting, because a normal woman might be more worried about her safety after a heated kiss.

Except she wanted to kiss him again.

She inwardly shook her head at her foolishness.

Zack grimaced and lifted his hand in a wave as he rolled backward out of the driveway. She stood on the lawn, shielding her eyes from the sun, her heart heavy and aching as she watched him drive away.

She felt something soft brush against her side and glanced down in surprise to see Lexi standing close, they way she usually stood next to her father. It was as if the little girl knew Julie was feeling sad again and wanted to offer comfort.

Her throat tightened with unshed tears, so she simply gave Lexi a hug. But when she glanced up, she noticed Derek was watching them with a frown.

She immediately released the little girl and stepped back, feeling as if she'd crossed a line. Why didn't Derek want her to be close to Lexi? Because they were leaving soon? Probably. She pulled herself together with an effort. "I better start dinner," she said in a low voice.

Derek didn't say anything as she went over to her side of the townhouse, closing the door firmly behind her.

She leaned weakly against the door, blinking back ridiculous tears. Why did she allow herself to get so emotionally involved? You would think she'd have learned her lesson with Andrew. She knew better than anyone how care and compassion did not lead to love.

Besides, she knew Derek and his daughter were only here for a brief stay. His unexpected kiss hadn't meant anything, except maybe to thank her.

After Andrew's betrayal, she'd refused to date. Well, to be fair, there hadn't been many available men to date. And she was afraid of making the same mistakes all over again.

Was she really willing to risk opening her heart to a man who'd made it clear he was just passing through?

No, she wasn't. With renewed strength and determination, she pushed away from the door and headed toward the fridge, where she'd stored the groceries she'd purchased that morning. She pulled out the chicken and searched for her skewer so she could make rotisserie chicken on the grill. Once the chicken was roasting away, she headed outside to her small garden to pick fresh lettuce, tomatoes, and cucumbers for the salad.

Puttering in her garden helped her to relax. Once she was sure she'd regained her composure, she went over to Derek and Lexi's side of the townhouse to see what they were up to and to let them know what time to expect dinner.

Her jaw dropped in surprise when she discovered Derek

was standing next to his packed suitcases while Lexi was rocking back and forth in the corner. "Where are you going?"

The flash of guilt in his eyes confirmed her worst fears. "Isn't it obvious? Your brother is worried about you, and I really don't blame him. I think it's best for everyone if Lexi and I move on."

"Why? How? You don't even have a car!"

"I know I've already imposed enough, but would you mind dropping us off at Billy's? Harold said he'd rent me a car cheap if needed. If you don't want to drive us, that's fine. We can walk. It's not that far."

"Don't go," she pleaded. "Not yet. Not until you're feeling better." Her earlier pep talk vanished in a puff of smoke now that she was faced with the reality of Derek's intent to leave. "Please?"

He hesitated, looking more worn out than ever before. "It's really best if we go."

It took all her willpower not to point out that leaving wasn't best for Lexi. The girl was rocking back and forth, staring at the floor, obviously upset. She wanted to go over and cuddle the girl close.

Was Lexi the reason Derek was so set on leaving? Because she was bonding too much with his daughter? She couldn't blame him for wanting to protect Lexi.

"If you really want to leave, it's best to wait until the morning. That way you'll have a whole day to travel, rather than just a few hours." Did she sound as desperate as she felt? Somehow she couldn't manage to drum up the energy to care. "And it's one less night you'll have to pay for a hotel room. Not to mention, I've already started dinner."

Derek stood indecisively, a deep frown furrowed in his brow as he rubbed a hand over his ribs. She imagined the pain was much worse now, considering the amount of work he'd done on the ceiling of her townhouse.

"Lexi, do you like chicken?" she asked. "Chicken roasted on the grill is one of my favorites. Dinner should be ready in less than a half hour."

"All right," Derek muttered with a sigh. "We'll stay one more night."

She felt relieved even though she knew the morning would be here soon enough. "Great. Do you need help putting the suitcases away?"

"No, but thanks," he said with a weary smile.

Since she still had the urge to comfort Lexi, she forced herself to turn around and leave. Derek had made his feelings known, leaving her little choice but to honor his wishes.

As she cleaned the vegetables from her garden, she couldn't help trying to think of a way to make Derek change his mind about leaving in the morning.

———————

DEREK ROLLED the suitcases back to the bedroom he shared with Lexi, wincing at how sore his muscles were. He hadn't felt this bad since waking up in the emergency department of Hope County Hospital.

And he'd hurt Julie's feelings too, but it couldn't be helped. Staying one more night wasn't smart, even if her logic made sense. Lexi's constant rocking was what had convinced him in the end. He couldn't bear to drag his daughter out of the townhouse kicking and screaming.

Hopefully Lexi would be better by tomorrow morning,

or he might not have a choice. Right now, he imagined Julie's cop brother was already running a check on him. Normally, he wouldn't be worried—after all, he didn't have a criminal record.

But Claire's parents were rather irrational in their quest for custody. They truly believed he was incapable of raising his own daughter. They'd demanded he hand Lexi over, and when he'd refused, things had turned ugly.

Threats, outrageous accusations—he'd been shocked at how bitterly angry they'd been.

He sank down on the edge of his bed and debated taking a pain pill. Working on the ceiling after finishing the walls had obviously been incredibly stupid. A hint of a smile tugged at his mouth as he remembered Julie calling him a stubborn ox.

Yeah, okay, so maybe he was a stubborn ox. Right now he was a hurting stubborn ox. But the last thing he wanted was for Julie to know how horrible he felt. She'd feel obligated to take him back to the hospital when all he really needed was a little rest. Or maybe a lot of rest.

Surely he could hang on long enough to eat dinner?

Of course he could. Soldiers could do anything.

"Daddy?" Lexi's fearful voice snapped him back into focus.

"Hey, baby-doll, what's up? Are you finished with your drawing?"

Lexi stared at him as if to ask who he was kidding. She'd been rocking since he'd explained how they needed to leave. Granted, he knew she might be sad to go, but he'd seriously underestimated her reaction.

For a moment, he doubted his ability to be a good father to Lexi. Maybe Claire's parents were right? Maybe she'd do better in the long run with more structure?

Maybe he was the idiot for thinking he knew what was best for Lexi?

"Hurts?" his daughter asked, coming close enough to put her tiny hand on his chest. He stared down at her for a long minute, choked up by her concern.

"Not too bad," he murmured. He reached up and tucked a glossy strand of hair behind her ear. "Are you still mad at me?"

Lexi shrugged and shook her head. "I love you, Daddy."

Her soft words arrowed straight into his heart. It was as if she knew exactly what he needed to hear.

"I love you too, baby-doll," he managed, drawing her close and gently resting his cheek on her hair. And suddenly, he knew that it was more than just Lexi knowing what he needed to hear.

It was God guiding him on the path he was supposed to take.

Feeling stronger, he pressed a kiss on top of Lexi's head and then struggled back to his feet, barely able to suppress a low groan. No doubt about it, he was going to be in a lot of pain tonight.

He forced himself to straighten his spine to walk down the hall into the gutted kitchen and living room. He held the patio door open for Lexi before following her outside to the patio.

Julie closed the hood of the grill and turned toward them. "I think I must have set the gas too high, because the chicken is just about done."

"I'm ready to eat whenever you are," he said as he lowered himself carefully into a chair. As much as he knew he should help Julie bring out the plates and silverware, he was afraid he'd only embarrass himself by falling flat on his face. "Lexi, would you please help Julie set the table?"

Lexi smiled and ran over to Julie. Soon they had the table set, complete with small salads.

Julie struggled a little with the roasted chicken, and he pushed himself up to help her. As they wrestled with the bird, Julie began to giggle. "This is why I don't do this more often," she said. "Too much work."

He carried the plate of roasted chicken out to the patio table. They all took their seats, but this time he decided to lead the prayer.

"Dear Lord, thank You for this wonderful food we're about to eat, and thank You for bringing Julie into our lives. Amen."

There was a half-second pause before Julie echoed, "Amen."

The food was delicious, but he must not have hidden the extent of his pain very well, because the moment they were finished, Julie jumped up. "Stay put, Derek. I'm going to get you some ibuprofen."

"Thanks." Maybe with the ibuprofen and the pain meds, he'd get some rest.

"Here you go," Julie said, dropping four tablets into the palm of his hand. The brush of her fingertips was so gentle he had the insane urge to kiss her again.

Bad idea, buddy, he told himself sternly. Really bad idea.

Lexi didn't have to be told to help Julie clear the table; she seemed actually eager for the task. Sitting and letting others do the work wasn't easy, but he stayed where he was, closing his eyes and hoping the ibuprofen would start to work.

Soon.

"Derek, why don't you go lie down?" Julie said. "You don't look comfortable sitting upright with your head tilted over to the side."

He grimaced and rubbed the crick in his neck. "It's too early for Lexi to go to bed."

"I know you don't want her to get too close to me," Julie said in a low voice, "but I thought we could light some sparklers tonight. I was saving them for the holiday, but if you're leaving in the morning, there's no point in waiting." Her sad smile made him feel even worse. "Get some rest, Derek. I'll bring Lexi in soon."

"Okay." He gritted his teeth and pushed himself upright. Julie slid her arm around his waist and helped keep him steady as he made his way inside.

"Take another pain pill," she ordered.

He was too sore to argue. "Thanks again," he murmured as he stretched out on the bed. Within minutes, he was sound asleep.

————

JULIE LIT SPARKLERS WITH LEXI, enjoying the way the little girl made sparkly circles by waving her arms. As they enjoyed the pre-holiday celebration, she tried not to dwell on the fact that Derek and Lexi were leaving in the morning.

Hearing Derek give the before-dinner prayer had been bittersweet. His gratitude had warmed her heart, even though she knew he was really just saying goodbye.

When Lexi began yawning, she put the sparklers away and gathered up the burnt sticks, making sure there weren't any glowing embers left over that might start a fire. The year before, they'd had a terrible drought, and the sheriff had put a ban on all fireworks, including sparklers. But this year had seen more snow and rain, allowing the citizens of Crystal

Lake to celebrate the Fourth of July holiday with all the usual fun and flair.

"Time for bed, Lexi," she said.

Surprisingly, the little girl didn't put up much of a fuss. Julie slid open the patio door so Lexi could step in.

The interior was dark, since there weren't any lights in the kitchen or living area. Julie felt along the wall to find the light switch.

"Brush your teeth and go to the bathroom, okay, Lexi?" she whispered.

"Okay." Lexi disappeared into the bathroom.

Julie leaned against the wall but then straightened when she heard a low groan. Derek? She walked farther down the hall until she reached the bedroom.

The door was ajar, and when she peeked in, she saw Derek writhing on the bed in pain, his hand on his chest as he fought against what looked to be a terrible muscle spasm.

9

J ulie couldn't ignore his pain, so she pushed the
door open and hurried into the room. "Easy now,"
she murmured, placing her hands on his chest and
pressing down on the muscles. "Let me try to help."

Derek let out another low groan, and she knew that even
though deep massage was the best way to ease the muscle
spasm, it was also painful.

"I'm sorry," she whispered even as she continued
pressing on his chest. His muscles felt rock hard beneath the
palms of her hands, and she felt awful knowing she was
hurting him. "Can you turn onto your side?"

He turned over so that his back was facing her, and she
continued to massage the tense muscles for him. Lexi came
up to stand beside her, looking anxiously at her father. Julie
tried to flash a reassuring smile. "Your daddy will be fine in
a few minutes. How about if you crawl into bed, okay,
sweetie?"

Lexi didn't say much but did as Julie suggested. She
knew Derek must be hurting very badly since he hadn't

tried to reassure his daughter the way he had in the emergency room.

She ignored the straining in her arms and shoulders as she continued her massage. The minutes slipped endlessly by until she felt the muscles in Derek's body begin to loosen up. But still, she didn't stop, for fear the muscles might tighten up again.

Another fifteen minutes later, Derek's breathing evened out, telling her the worst was over. The muscles beneath her fingers were finally relaxed and supple. "You're amazing," he murmured.

A reluctant smile tugged at her mouth. "Hardly. I'm a nurse, remember?"

"And an excellent one, at that. Thanks, Julie," Derek said in a low voice. He rolled onto his back, gently taking her hands in his, giving them a quick squeeze. "I'm feeling much better now."

When he let go, she stepped back, gently flexing her own wrists and elbows. "Are you sure?"

"Yes." As if to prove his point, he rolled upright so that he was sitting on the edge of the bed. He gingerly ran his hand down his chest. "I was an idiot. You have every right to say 'I told you so,'" he muttered.

She let out a heavy sigh. "There's no point. You obviously figured that out the hard way."

"Yeah, that's true. Is Lexi okay?"

"Looks like she's asleep," she said, taking a step back so that he could see his daughter. "Do you want another pain pill before I go?"

"It's too soon. Besides, I'll be fine."

His evasive tone made her wonder if he even had any pain medicine left. But it was too late to go out now, especially on a Sunday. "We'll get your prescription filled tomorrow."

He grimaced and avoided her gaze. "I'll be fine," he repeated. "Goodnight, Julie. Thanks again for making me feel better."

She wanted to try and convince him not to leave in the morning, but it was getting late, and she didn't want to disturb Lexi's sleep, so she let it go. "Goodnight, Derek."

Julie tiptoed out of the room and gently closed the door behind her. She walked through the gutted kitchen and living area, thinking about how Derek had overworked himself earlier that afternoon. The night air was cool as she went outside. The quiet night soothed her soul, and she stopped for a moment and tipped her head back to gaze up at the stars.

Please, Lord, show Derek the path You want him to take. Amen.

————————

DEREK WOKE up to bright sunlight streaming in through the window, betraying the fact he'd overslept. For a moment, he was almost afraid to move, but his stomach rumbled, reminding him he hadn't eaten much the night before. He gingerly tested his muscles, noting that he was still a bit stiff and sore, although nothing like the agonizing pain of last night. He glanced over to find his daughter, but Lexi was already up and gone. No doubt, she'd gone over to eat breakfast with Julie.

Julie. For a moment, he closed his eyes, remembering

how she'd helped him out last night, easing his pain. He was indebted to her again. Big-time.

And how was he going to make it up to her? By leaving.

A wave of regret washed over him. He didn't want to leave. Didn't want to go back to driving through towns filled with strangers.

But if he stayed, he risked being discovered, either by her brother, Zack, doing a background check on him, or by the Hope County deputy who was likely filing his accident report today.

With a heavy heart, he climbed out of bed and headed into the bathroom. He found the waterproof dressings and realized a hot shower would help him feel better. At least physically, if not emotionally.

The steamy water did wonders for his sore muscles, but his mind still whirled with indecision. He was no closer to a solution as he dressed and headed over to find Lexi and hopefully some breakfast.

He found his daughter crouching in the garden next to Julie, listening intently as Julie showed her how to pull weeds. He blinked to make sure he wasn't hallucinating, but no, his daughter was actually doing something besides drawing and playing video games.

Because of Julie—not because of him.

The kernel of self-doubt he'd experienced the day before abruptly grew to astronomical proportions. Was he really doing the right thing for Lexi? Maybe he wasn't cut out to be a single father.

"Daddy!" Lexi caught sight of him and came over to wrap her arms around his waist. Her fingers were coated with dirt, but he didn't care as he hugged her back. "Better?" she asked, tipping her head back to look up at him.

"Much better, baby-doll. It's nice of you to help Julie with her garden."

"Tomatoes," Lexi said with a gleam in her eye. "I like tomatoes."

"They're my favorite, too," Julie said, swiping her hands down the sides of her jeans. Her smile didn't quite meet her eyes. "You're looking better, Derek. Are you hungry? We had French toast this morning."

"I am hungry, but you don't have to wait on me," he said in a rush. "I can make my own breakfast."

"I don't mind. Just give me a minute to wash up. Lexi? Come with me. You need to wash your hands, too."

Lexi gave a nod and skipped next to Julie as they went inside. He let out his breath in a heavy sigh and followed more slowly. He sank down into the closest kitchen chair and held his head in his hands.

Help me, Lord. Guide me. Show me the way.

"Derek? Are you all right?" Julie asked, putting her hand on his shoulder. He had to stop himself from taking her hand in his and pulling her close.

"Fine," he said gruffly. "Where's Lexi?"

"She went outside to draw." Her brow was pulled into a frown. "You don't look fine, Derek. You look like you're still in pain."

He was, but not the kind of pain she was talking about. "Really, I'm fine."

"I'll get you more ibuprofen, but you shouldn't take it on an empty stomach." Julie took her hand away and went back over to where she had the ingredients assembled for breakfast. "This won't take long."

"I'm not leaving." The words popped out of his mouth before he even realized he was going to say them.

She froze, looking a little ridiculous with the spatula hanging in mid-air. "You're not?"

A smile tugged at the corner of his mouth. "No, I'm not. Unless you want me to."

"I...no." For a moment, she gaped at him. "Why would you think I wanted you to leave?"

He didn't know why he had the insane urge to confide in Julie. He forced himself to hold back the instinct. "I thought maybe your brother might have talked you into it."

"No, of course not." She flipped the egg-coated bread on the sizzling grill. "We lost our parents several years ago, and Zack tends to be a bit on the overprotective side. But he's been more withdrawn and abrupt these days, ever since he lost his daughter to leukemia eighteen months ago."

His chest tightened with sympathy. He couldn't imagine losing Lexi to some horrible cancer. And now that he knew, he could understand why her brother had wanted to get far away yesterday. "That's tough. I can't say that I blame him."

"Yes, it's been difficult." Julie stared at the French toast, but he sensed she was really looking back into the past. "Amelia was a beautiful little girl. Constantly talking, constantly moving. Until she got sick..." Her voice trailed off.

He pushed to his feet. "I'm sorry, Julie. Why don't I take over here? You should sit down for a while."

"No, it's all right." Her smile was pathetic, but he gave her points for trying. "When I first saw Lexi, she reminded me a little of Amelia, but they're really very different."

He straightened, ready to come to Lexi's defense. But he needn't have worried.

"Lexi is so quiet and so talented. She's the complete opposite of Amelia. Every time Lexi draws another picture for me, I'm flabbergasted at how good she really is. You might want to consider getting her into an art program."

"I have thought about it," he agreed. Too bad art programs were expensive and he was currently unemployed. But he was determined not to be unemployed forever. And he ignored the tiny voice in his head telling him Claire's parents would be able to afford an art program. They believed that super-strict private school was best for Lexi. There was no way they'd even consider paying for an art program.

"Sit down, Derek, these will be ready shortly."

He reluctantly returned to the table, yet despite the seriousness of the conversation and his conflicting thoughts, he felt lighter, less apprehensive than he had when he'd first woken up.

Because he'd agreed to stay. A decision he'd made for himself as much as for his daughter.

———

JULIE WAS SECRETLY THRILLED Derek wasn't leaving, but she tried to hold her emotions in check. After all, he'd leave eventually.

Unless, of course, he found a reason to stay?

Ridiculous to allow her thoughts to wander down that path. She sensed Derek didn't have a lot of money, and the way he'd asked about any manufacturing jobs made her more convinced that he needed work of some sort.

He was doing a great job on her townhouse, but after he'd overexerted himself yesterday, she didn't want him anywhere near a crowbar or a hammer. If he would just give himself time to heal, they could probably come to some sort of arrangement.

So what was his hurry?

She had no idea. Unless he was walking the edge financially, which was a distinct possibility. At least his appetite had returned.

"I have to work a four-hour shift this afternoon," she said, crossing over to join him at the table. "Apparently, one of the nurses called in sick, so they've asked me to cover from three to seven-thirty."

"No problem," Derek said. "Lexi and I will be fine."

"Why don't we stop by and pick up your accident report?" she offered. "That way you can get your insurance company focused on getting your settlement ready."

Derek stared down at his plate for a moment, and she wondered if he resented the fact that she was poking her nose into his business. But really, it was silly of him to rent some car when the insurance company needed to pay him for the wrecked vehicle.

Unless he hadn't been telling the truth about having insurance?

"All right," Derek agreed.

She was surprised but pleased. "Great. We'll head out as soon as I'm finished."

"No, we'll head out as soon as I finish the dishes," he corrected. "You cooked, so it's my job to clean up."

She was about to protest but then realized that Derek probably needed to feel as if he were contributing at least in some way. And since working on the townhouse wasn't an option, doing the dishes was a dismal second. "All right, I'll see what Lexi is up to."

Lexi was drawing another picture of the lake, only this time, she focused more on the boats and skiers rather than on the trees and water. Julie sat down next to her. "Who taught you how to draw, Lexi?"

"Mommy," Lexi responded absently, barely looking up from her picture.

This was the first time Lexi had mentioned her mother, and Julie sensed she should tread lightly. "That's wonderful," she murmured.

"I miss my Mommy," Lexi said plaintively.

She didn't want to assume that Lexi's mother died, so she wrapped her arm around the little girl's shoulders in a soft hug. "What happened, sweetie?"

"My mommy died." Lexi abruptly dropped her pencil and turned to bury her face against her breast.

"Oh, sweetie, I'm sorry," she murmured, her heart aching for the child. "But I'm sure your mommy is up in heaven with God."

Lexi lifted her head, her tiny face intense as she absorbed the idea. "You mean like an angel?"

She nodded. "Yes, exactly like an angel. Every time you miss her, you should just close your eyes and talk to her. I'm sure she's an angel up in heaven listening to you."

"Really?" Lexi's voice held a hint of hope mixed with doubt.

"I promise," she murmured, tears welling in her eyes as she glanced over to see Derek hovering in the doorway. Would he be upset that she'd talked to Lexi about heaven and God? She hoped not.

"Julie is right, Lexi," he said as he walked outside. "Your mommy is up in heaven with God."

The little girl smiled and released Julie in favor of her father. Derek scooped her up and held her close as Julie discreetly swiped at her damp eyes.

"Are you ready to go?" Derek asked after he set Lexi back down.

"Sure." It was almost as if Derek wanted to get the

errand over with. Not that she could blame him. Maybe he thought that the sooner he put his insurance company on notice, the sooner he could get a replacement vehicle.

And the sooner he could leave, taking Lexi far away.

The ride to the sheriff's department took about fifteen minutes, and as she drove into the parking lot, Derek's expression grew grim, and she half-expected him to ask her to turn around.

They climbed out of the car and into the hot, humid air. The sun reflected off the blacktop parking lot as they made their way toward the building. The interior of the building was much cooler in comparison, the blast of air-conditioning causing her to feel chilled.

"Hi, Grace, how are you?" she greeted the older woman who sat behind the dispatch desk.

"Hanging in there," Grace responded with a grimace. She was a large woman, her dark hair liberally streaked with gray. "Stay back, Julie, I might have a touch of the flu. I've been feeling sick to my stomach, and my back's been hurting too. Gotta tell you, getting old sure ain't fun."

Now that Grace mentioned being in pain, Julie noticed that her skin was ashen with tiny brackets of pain lining her mouth. "Maybe you should have called in sick today," Julie suggested with a frown. "You look like you could use some rest."

"Carol had her baby last night," Grace said with a heavy sigh. "Leaves us only four dispatchers for a while, and we've gotta cover all three shifts. But that's enough about me. What can I do for you?"

She still didn't think Grace looked so good, but she introduced Derek. "Derek needs a copy of his accident report from Friday evening, so that he can get in touch with his insurance company."

"Oh yeah, heard all about that from Deputy Thomas, especially after he arrested that no-good Tommy Hinkle," Grace said. She struggled to her feet and then braced herself against the desk, as if she couldn't get her breath.

Something was definitely wrong. Julie hurried around through the open doorway to Grace. The woman was sweating profusely, and her skin had gone slate gray.

"Sit down, Grace." She glanced back at Derek. "She needs an ambulance. We need to call 911, but Grace is the one who usually takes those emergency calls." It was crazy to think that she couldn't get help for the dispatcher.

Derek had followed her inside the dispatch office. "I know how to use the radio," he said as he took over the controls.

"Grace, try to take slow, deep breaths," Julie said, suspecting the dispatcher was having a heart attack right before her eyes. "Do you have a baby aspirin in your purse?"

"No," Grace answered weakly.

She bit her lip and listened as Derek confidently put out the 911 call, praying help would arrive soon.

But then Grace slumped in her seat, and she knew there wasn't a moment to waste. "Help me get her to the floor," she said to Derek. "I need to start CPR."

10

As an ER nurse, this wasn't the first time she'd had to perform CPR, but providing life-saving measures in the middle of the dispatch office was much different than being in the emergency room where they had equipment readily available. What she wouldn't give for an oxygen tank, ambu mask, and meds.

"I can help," Derek murmured, kneeling on the opposite side of Grace's prone figure. He gently tipped her head back so he could provide rescue breaths as needed.

Julie was extremely grateful for Derek's support. She spared Lexi a quick glance, noting the little girl was off to the side, watching them with wide blue eyes. Julie's heart went out to the child, but she couldn't allow herself to be distracted.

"One and two and three and," she counted out loud for Derek's benefit. They worked in tandem through two rounds of CPR before Derek insisted they switch places.

Shortly after the switch, two Deputies came rushing in. "What happened to Grace?" Deputy Matson demanded.

"Heart attack. Where's the ambulance?" Julie asked. She recognized both deputies from working in the ER.

"On the way," Deputy Armbruster said. He swept his gaze around the interior of the office. "Poor Grace. We must have overworked her, and it's even worse now that Carol delivered her baby."

"Yeah," Deputy Matson agreed. "But we need to find someone to take her place, and quick." Even as he spoke, he leaned over to take a call.

"Derek knows how," she said before leaning down to give two rescue breaths.

"Really?" Deputy Armbruster asked hopefully.

Derek appeared to be concentrating on nothing more than doing good chest compressions. And doing an excellent job, based on the strength of Grace's pulse.

Please, take care of Grace, Lord!

The wailing sounds of the ambulance made her weak with relief. Within moments, the paramedics were inside the building, coming over with a gurney, heart monitor, and supplies. She'd never been so thankful for medical supplies.

Derek continued chest compressions, and Julie gave another two breaths before looking up at the paramedics. "I suspect she's having an acute myocardial infarction."

"What were her symptoms?" The first paramedic wore a nametag that said Sam. He nudged Derek aside in order to place large patches on Grace's chest. Within seconds, he had her hooked up to the portable cardiac monitor.

"Pale, sweating, complaints of back pain and nausea," she said as she watched Grace's heart rhythm. "She's in v-fib."

"All clear! Shocking at 200 joules," Sam said as he pushed the button on the machine.

She watched Sam give two more shocks, and then

suddenly, Grace's heart rhythm changed into what looked to be a normal sinus rhythm with depressed ST segments. Julie leaned forward to feel for a pulse. She felt a rush of relief when she found the thready beat. "We have a pulse."

"Let's give more oxygen and nitro so that we can get her packed up to roll," Sam said to the other paramedic. "We need to get to the hospital before we lose her again."

Julie rose to her feet and backed away, knowing there wasn't anything more she could do. She glanced over to find Derek hugging Lexi and wondered if seeing Grace had reminded the little girl about losing her mother.

She sent off another prayer for Grace, hoping the dispatcher would be all right. Now that the adrenalin rush was over, she felt shaky and weak.

After the paramedics left, there was a weird silence in the dispatch area as if no one knew what to say next. "Thanks for your help," Deputy Armbruster finally said. "I'm thankful you were both here for Grace. Your quick thinking made all the difference."

"Glad we could help," Derek murmured.

Julie tried to smile. "Derek saved the day. I wasn't sure how we were going to call for help, but he jumped right in."

The deputy nodded and then cleared his throat. "Were you serious about knowing how to do dispatch?"

Derek shrugged and nodded, still keeping his arm around Lexi. "Yeah, I learned in the Army."

"Would you consider a temporary job for the summer?" Armbruster asked. "Obviously, we could use some help around here. With both Grace and Carol on medical leave, we're really strapped for help. I can put in a good word with Sheriff Torretti once you fill out an application."

Julie held her breath, waiting for Derek's reply.

"I'd very much like a job, even a temporary one," Derek said. "If you're serious about hiring me."

She closed her eyes with relief. *Thank You, Lord!*

———

DEREK KNEW he was crazy to even consider taking a job with the Hope County Sheriff's Department. The risk was too high. But the lure of paid employment was too much to ignore. Since no one had come to arrest him, he had to assume his background check had been fine. Claire's parents must not have sent the police after him, despite his fears. Or maybe hiring a private investigator was more their style, especially since he was Lexi's legal guardian.

For now.

He couldn't help thinking that this potential job was a sign from God. He'd considered settling down somewhere to establish himself as part of a community, so why not here in Crystal Lake? Wiping his damp palms on the sides of his jeans, he sat down in front of the computer.

"I'll pick up your police report while we're waiting," Julie said, her eyes bright with excitement. She took Lexi by the hand and went over to talk with Deputy Armbruster.

Calling himself all kinds of a fool for taking the risk, he began filling out the online application form. His longest work experience was the eight years in the Army, but he also put in the technical college degree and the construction work he'd done prior to that.

When it came to references, he stared blankly at the screen. Claire's parents were out of the question. After a long moment, he put in his CO's name and number, along with Jake Strawn, his Chicago buddy's name and number. Lastly, he put in Julie's name and then felt foolish when he realized he didn't have her number.

When he was finished, he pushed the send button and stood up. He glanced over to the two deputies. "I put in my cell number, and I'm staying in Julie Crain's rehabbed townhouse if you need to get in touch with me."

"Sounds good. Thanks again," Deputy Armstrong said, offering his hand.

It was surreal to shake the deputy's hand before walking outside to meet Julie and Lexi.

"Julie said we can get ice cream," Lexi announced. "Can I have chocolate, Daddy?"

"Ice cream, huh?" he asked, sending Julie a wry smile.

"Well, why not? We're celebrating, aren't we?" Julie asked cheerfully. "I called into the ER, and Grace has been taken straight to the cardiac cath lab. They told me she was critical but stable, and her chances look fairly good at this point. And you have a new job. Two very good reasons to celebrate."

"I haven't been offered the job yet," he reminded her. Although it surprised him how keenly he wanted it. He grinned at Lexi. "Yes, Lexi, chocolate ice cream sounds good to me, too."

They left Julie's car in the small parking lot and walked down the couple of blocks to Main Street. The summer sun was hot but not nearly as bad as what they'd suffered in Afghanistan. For a moment, he imagined himself back there, holding on to his rifle with a tight, sweaty grip as he stayed alert, searching for signs of Afghani soldiers. He shook his head to dislodge the painful memory and forced himself to glance around curiously. There were lots of cars and people crowding the street, which wasn't surprising since he'd been unable to find a hotel with a vacancy over the holiday weekend. Still, being surrounded by families made him acutely aware of the way he, Julie, and Lexi fit right in.

Don't go there, he warned himself. They were not a family. It would do well to remember Julie was being a friend to him, nothing more.

The ice cream parlor was packed, so they patiently waited their turn. They all three ended up with chocolate ice cream, but when Julie pulled out her purse, he stopped her with a hand on her arm. "I've got it."

When she looked as if she were about to protest, he narrowed his gaze, shook his head, and fished out his wallet. After he paid for the cones, they strolled back outside.

"There's a Fourth of July parade here tomorrow morning," Julie said. "I have to work a twelve-hour shift, but you and Lexi should come and watch."

"Would you like that, Lexi?" he asked, glancing down at his daughter's chocolate-smeared face.

She nodded vigorously, too preoccupied with her ice cream to say anything.

"If you want to borrow my car, you can drop me off at work in the morning," Julie continued. "Although I should warn you I need to be at the hospital by seven a.m."

"Not a problem," he murmured. He glanced around, wondering if this was real or little more than an incredible dream. He'd been on edge ever since leaving St. Louis, to the point he'd been unable to relax. Being here now, walking down Main Street with Julie and Lexi, he felt comfortable and at ease.

He told himself that he was taking the risk of staying here for Lexi's sake. Because his daughter seemed to be happy. And he couldn't bear the thought of hauling Lexi out of Julie's townhouse against her will.

But deep down, he suspected he was really staying for himself. As much as he liked the town of Crystal Lake, he liked Julie Crain even more.

———

JULIE KNEW they were attracting some attention from the locals as they made their way through town but couldn't bring herself to care. Derek was staying. He and Lexi were staying!

She knew Derek would be offered a job with the sheriff's department and hoped and prayed he'd accept. Things were working out perfectly. It was almost as if coming in last night to find Derek's packed suitcases hadn't happened.

"Are you ready to head back?" she asked Derek as the crowds of people became suffocating. She understood the town depended on tourism to survive, but she preferred the quiet days when there weren't so many strangers around.

"Sure," Derek agreed.

She had some time yet before she had to go into work, and she found herself wishing she hadn't agreed to help out. At least she was only filling in for four hours, and the extra money would come in handy. Especially once Derek was ready to begin putting up new drywall.

The thought pulled her up short. There was no guarantee that Derek would stay with her once he was offered a dispatch job with the sheriff's department. He might insist on moving somewhere else. Although surely he'd still need her help to watch Lexi while he was working, wouldn't he? Her mind spun with the logistics.

Obviously, they needed to talk once the job offer came through, but for now, she decided to take each day one at a time.

When they arrived back at the townhouse, Lexi wanted to go back out on the boat.

Julie glanced at the clock. "Sure, we can go out for an hour or so before I have to leave for work."

"Yay!"

Julie smiled, glad to see Lexi jump from one foot to another with excitement. The shy little girl who'd come from the accident scene was slowly fading away.

"Okay, let's get your swimming suit," Derek said, taking Lexi by the hand.

"Don't forget your waterproof dressings," Julie added.

"I won't."

Within fifteen minutes, they were down on Zack's boat. Julie held out the keys for Derek. "Do you want to drive?"

"Sure." His eyes gleamed with anticipation, which made her laugh as she took a seat toward the front of the boat.

Dozens of other boaters were on the lake as well, but Derek did a fine job of steering clear of everyone else. "I should have inflated the inner tube for Lexi," Julie said with a wry glance over her shoulder at Derek. "I have everything beneath the seat cushion but didn't even think to use the pump to inflate the inner tube."

"Next time," he said easily.

She sat back against the seat, thinking about how happy she was to know there would be a next time. She tipped her face into the sun and thought about how wonderful it was to be outside like this.

But all too soon, it was time to head into shore. She

changed into her scrubs and then left for work with Derek's promise to have dinner ready by the time she came home ringing through her ears. She couldn't help the broad smile that seemed permanently grooved into her cheeks as she entered the busy ER.

"What is up with you?" Merry greeted her with a smile. "It's been a long time since I've seen you so happy."

Julie knew Merry was referring to her sorrow over losing Amelia and her broken engagement. It wasn't as if she'd tried to wallow in the past, but watching her young niece pass away had been the hardest thing she'd ever done. Much harder than suffering through the gossip of Andrew's affair. She'd leaned on God and prayer, but for some reason, it had taken being with Derek and Lexi to pull her back to normal. "I am happy," she responded lightly. "Have you been busy here?"

"You could say that," Merry said with a sigh. "If you could take team one and the trauma bay, I'd appreciate it."

"Sure thing. Fill me in on the patients who are in team one."

Within minutes, she was swept away into the controlled chaos of the emergency department. Her cell phone rang, but she was busy admitting another patient, so she ignored it. When she had a break, she noticed the call was from her brother and made a mental note to call him back when her shift was over.

"How's Grace Banner doing?" she asked Merry when they crossed paths.

"She's doing great. She had two cardiac stents put in but thankfully didn't need open-heart surgery."

"I'm so glad to hear that," Julie murmured. "I was really afraid she wouldn't do well."

"Everyone around here has been saying that Grace is

alive today because of you," Merry informed her. "If you hadn't been at the sheriff's department to start CPR, it's likely she wouldn't have made it."

Since Grace had been alone in the dispatch center, Julie knew Merry was probably right. "Derek is the true hero," she said. "He used the radio to call for help, and his chest compressions were far better than mine."

Merry raised a brow. "Derek, huh? Would that be Mr. Derek Ryerson and his adorable daughter, Lexi?"

She blushed and nodded. "You know very well that's him."

Merry reached out to put a gentle hand on Julie's arm. "Jules, be careful, okay? I know he seems like a nice guy, but after everything you've been through in the past year, I don't think it's wise to jump into anything."

The memory of Derek's kiss warmed her cheeks. "Don't worry, I'm not jumping into anything. We're friends, that's all. And I'm hoping to bring him back to the church."

Merry's eyes were shadowed with worry. "While getting him to come back to his faith is great, just remember you felt the same way about Andrew, and look how that ended up."

"I know." Andrew had also come through the ER after a waterskiing accident, which had broken his left tibia and fibula. She'd reached out to him and offered her help, which he'd gratefully accepted. They'd grown close over the next few months, and he'd even proposed marriage, which had thrilled her. But then she'd discovered his old girlfriend had come to town and that Rebecca had stayed overnight at his place for the weekend. When she'd confronted Andrew, he'd told her it was her fault because she wouldn't sleep with him. And he made it clear that he was only going along with her ideas of faith and attending church because that was what she'd wanted.

News of Andrew's affair and their broken engagement had rippled through the town to the point she couldn't go anywhere without someone offering her sympathy. Only after Andrew and Rebecca had returned to Madison did the wagging tongues die down.

She pulled herself back from the painful memories. "I know, Merry, but it's different this time. Derek isn't Andrew."

"Maybe not, but he is new in town just like Andrew was. And really, what do you know about Derek on a personal level?"

Merry sounded just like her brother, Zack, which caused a rare flash of temper. "I know he's a stubborn, hard-working guy and a very good father. And I know he used to serve our country in the Army, too. Honestly, Merry, he's been nothing but polite and respectful."

"What about faith?" Merry persisted. "Don't make the same mistake you made with Andrew."

"Granted, Derek didn't attend church with me, but he participates in prayer, so I think there's hope." When Merry opened her mouth again, Julie held up her hand. "Don't, Merry. Derek and I are friends, nothing more. So leave it alone, okay?"

"Okay," Merry agreed with a sigh. Her pager went off, and she read the message with a grimace. "Looks like another ambulance is on the way in."

Julie returned to work, glancing frequently at the clock as the last hour of her shift passed by with excruciating slowness. When her co-worker came in to relieve her, she headed out to the parking lot, happy to be going home.

To see Derek. And of course, Lexi.

True to his word, Derek had brats and hotdogs ready for

the grill when she arrived. "Smells delicious," she said as she stepped out on the patio.

"It's nothing fancy," Derek said. "Although I did make potato salad, too."

"Wow, a man who can cook," she said lightly, Merry's concern echoing in her mind. Was she reading too much into Derek's kindness? Was it possible this was all just a big act he was putting on for her benefit?

"Sit down. I'll bring the food over in a minute," Derek said. The relaxed smile on his face only emphasized his handsome looks. If this really was an act, the guy deserved an Academy Award.

Derek brought the tray of food over and set it in the center of the table. When they were all seated, Julie bowed her head to pray. "Dear Lord, thank You so much for providing us this food we are about to eat. Also, please keep watching over Grace as she heals in the hospital, as she very much needs Your strength and support. Amen."

"And please watch over Grandma and Grandpa, too," Lexi added. "Amen."

Grandma and Grandpa? Julie raised her head. The stricken expression on Derek's face confirmed he'd lied to her that night in the hospital about how he and Lexi were alone.

She felt sick to her stomach as she wondered what else he'd lied about.

11

D erek swallowed hard as Julie went pale, her gaze full of reproach as she stared at him. He couldn't very well chide Lexi for including her grandparents in their evening prayer, because for one thing, Claire's parents needed prayers in a big way. And for another, this abrupt revelation wasn't Lexi's fault.

It was his.

"I'll explain later," he murmured, trying to reassure Julie with a half-hearted smile.

Julie frowned but thankfully didn't say anything in front of Lexi. And he mentally kicked himself over and over again when Julie did little more than pick at her food.

He should have confided in her before now. Before she'd grown close to Lexi. Before they'd become friends.

Before he'd kissed her.

His own appetite vanished along with Julie's, but he made an effort for Lexi's sake. But no matter how hard he tried, there was no way to ease the strained atmosphere.

When they'd finally finished, he pushed his chair away from the table. "Lexi, help me clear the dishes," he said.

"I'll do it," Julie said abruptly, jumping to her feet. He sensed she wanted to get away and wished he could think of a way to make her realize...what? That he was sorry he'd led her to believe that he and Lexi were all alone in the world? That he hadn't intended to mislead her at all? That all he wanted was to help Lexi get out of that strict private school and recover from the shock of losing her mother?

For a moment, he dropped his head into his hands, feeling almost as helpless as the night Claire's parents had informed him they were going to take him to court in an attempt to gain custody of Lexi. He'd been completely alone then.

But somehow, he felt even worse now. Because despite everything Julie had done for them, he'd let her down.

Guide me through this, Lord. Show me the way.

When he felt Lexi's soft hand on his arm, he pulled himself together. His daughter's expression was troubled, and he wished more than anything for her to be happy again. The way she'd been on the boat ride or swimming in the lake. "I love you, Lexi," he said softly.

"I love you, too, Daddy." Instantly, Lexi was crawling into his lap, and he held her tightly, almost afraid to let her go.

After several long moments, he kissed the top of Lexi's head and eased away. "Come on, baby-doll, we need to help carry these dishes in for Julie." Since Julie hadn't returned after escaping inside, he figured it was the least they could do.

"Okay." Lexi grabbed the ketchup bottle with both hands as he stacked the rest of the dirty plates and they both went inside.

The kitchen was empty when he set the dirty dishes on the counter. Should he try to find Julie? Or give her the privacy she deserved?

As he went back outside to pick up the last of the dishes and condiments, his chest tightened with panic. What if Julie planned to ask him and Lexi to leave? She had every right to kick them out if she wanted to.

How much would her sweet, Christian nature tolerate? He suspected he'd already pushed her past the breaking point.

His thoughts whirled as he cleaned up the after-dinner mess. Since Julie was still nowhere to be found, he decided he should wash the dishes, too.

It was the least he could do to make amends.

Sensing he'd intruded enough, he left the dishes to air dry and made his way outside onto the patio. The sun was low on the horizon, and he wished Julie were here to share in the wonder of the beautiful sunset over the lake.

And then he saw her, sitting on the grassy bank of the lakeshore, hugging her knees to her chest. She must have gone out the front door and slipped down to the lake without his noticing.

He needed to talk to her even though it was too early to send Lexi to bed. Thankfully, his daughter happened to be preoccupied with a video game. "Stay here, okay, Lexi?"

She gave him a tiny nod.

Derek took a deep breath and let it out slowly as he walked down to talk to Julie.

————

JULIE HEARD Derek's footsteps swishing against the grass and mentally braced herself as he dropped down beside her.

"I'm sorry," he said in his deep, soft voice.

She didn't turn to look at him. "Your personal life is none of my business," she said in a frosty tone.

There was a brief pause, but she kept her gaze focused on the setting sun. She wasn't in the mood to talk, and hopefully, Derek would get the message and leave her alone.

"You already know Lexi's mother died about four months ago," he said. "I was still in Afghanistan, trying to fight through the red tape to return stateside when Claire told me she was diagnosed with pancreatic cancer. They gave her six months, but she didn't last that long. I missed her death by a full month, and by the time I returned, Claire's parents had taken over Lexi's care."

She couldn't pretend indifference to his story. "I'm sorry. That must have been awful for you."

He nodded and shrugged. "Even though I'd been gone for almost seven months, Lexi remembered me and latched onto me like I was her rock amidst the storm. Turns out that Claire's parents had very distinct ideas about childrearing, and in fact, they'd enrolled Lexi in a super-strict private school that she absolutely hated."

Her heart squeezed for the little girl. "At least there's no school in the summer," she murmured.

Derek let out a harsh laugh. "There was for Lexi. It was clear Claire's parents didn't want her underfoot all day, but when I took Lexi out of the program, they went nuts. Claimed I had no idea how to raise my own daughter. They were...so angry."

She glanced over, feeling sympathy for Derek and the awful situation he'd found himself in. "I'm sure they were just grieving their daughter," she said.

"Maybe," he allowed. "But you have to understand, they never liked me. Obviously because I was irresponsible enough to get their daughter pregnant but mostly because I was nothing more than a soldier in the Army. When I discovered Claire was pregnant, I begged her to marry me, but she refused. I'm sure the last thing her parents wanted was me as a son-in-law. I spent as much time with Lexi as I could and sent most of my paycheck to Claire to help pay for expenses. Right before I was deployed to Afghanistan, I thought Claire was softening toward me. That she might even give a more permanent relationship a try."

"What happened?"

"Four months into my deployment, she told me she had pancreatic cancer." Derek's expression was so bleak she longed to comfort him. "I couldn't believe it at first, because she seemed so healthy before I left."

She was all too familiar with the way cancer sneaked up and stole a life when you least expected it. "Pancreatic cancer is difficult to diagnose, and once you have symptoms, it's almost always too late."

Derek let out a heavy sigh. "Yeah, that's exactly what happened. Anyway, Claire begged me to look after Lexi when she was gone. She arranged for me to have custody and told me that Lexi needed her father more than ever now. I gave her my promise that I would."

"Oh, Derek," she murmured. "Of course you and Lexi belong together. I just don't understand why you didn't tell me this sooner?"

"You didn't let me finish," he said dryly. "I think Claire's parents expected me to drop Lexi into their laps and return to Afghanistan. When I told them I had custody of her, they were furious. Claire's parents are rich and prominent members of society. They're best friends with several judges. When they told me they would fight for custody and win, I believed them. So I cashed in what was left of my savings and took off with Lexi."

"Ohhh," she said as the picture became crystal clear. "So you're running away from Claire's parents."

"I'm protecting Lexi from Claire's parents," he corrected sharply. "They have this, I don't know, strange idea of what Lexi should be and are determined to mold her into their image of a perfect granddaughter. They buy her all kinds of frilly things and girl toys that Lexi could care less about. They just don't understand Lexi is perfect the way she is."

His defensiveness regarding Lexi made her want to smile. "Of course Lexi is perfect the way she is, but Derek, don't you think Claire's parents have a right to be a part of Lexi's life?"

"Not if they threaten to take her away from me," he muttered harshly.

She sighed and shook her head. "Derek, do you really think a judge, even one who might know Claire's parents, would take custody away from a child's biological father?"

"Yes, I do. Especially since the only job offer I had was from Claire's father, which, of course, magically disappeared when I took Lexi out of that ridiculous school." Anger shimmered in Derek's tone. "You can bet they'd take custody away from me in a heartbeat. Which is why I'm asking you to keep this quiet for now. I have to believe that Claire's parents didn't call the police on me yet, since Deputy Armbruster didn't seem at all suspicious. But I also think it's just a matter of time. And if I can get this job, then I'll be one step closer to keeping Lexi."

She had to admit his logic made sense. How could she deny him the opportunity to keep his daughter? Especially since she really didn't want him to leave.

For selfish reasons, not necessarily noble ones.

"I won't say anything," she promised.

Derek nodded and rose to his feet, still favoring his right

side as he placed a hand over the right side of his chest. "Thank you."

She watched him walk back to Lexi, hoping and praying that Derek wasn't still in love with Claire. Because she was already starting to care about him.

Far too much.

———————

AFTER A RESTLESS NIGHT, Julie dragged herself out of bed to get ready for her twelve-hour shift in the ER. A quick shower made her feel a little better, although she desperately needed coffee to kick-start her brain.

When she trudged into the kitchen, she was brought up short by the sight of Derek and Lexi sitting at her kitchen table eating bowls of cold cereal.

She blinked owlishly at them. "Good morning."

"Good morning." Derek's voice was tentative, as if unsure if she was still upset with him or not. "I made coffee. Hope you don't mind."

She forced a smile. "I could use about a gallon," she said, making her way over to the steaming pot. "Thanks."

Several sips later, the rush of caffeine cleared her mind. When she turned back toward the table, she realized there was a bowl and spoon already set out for her.

"Um, is the offer of driving you to work still an option?" Derek asked hesitantly. "I thought it would be nice to take Lexi to the parade, but we can always walk if you'd prefer."

"No need to walk, you can use the car today," she assured him. It wasn't necessary for him to keep tiptoeing around her, but she wasn't sure how to get their former camaraderie back. "We'll have to leave in about fifteen minutes, though."

"No problem. Finish your breakfast and leave the dishes. I'll take care of them."

She nodded, feeling a little bit like she was taking advantage of him, but there wasn't time to do anything about it now. As soon as she finished her breakfast, she stood and grabbed her stethoscope. "I'm ready."

Lexi must have been tired because she didn't say much as Derek drove the ten miles to Hope County Hospital. When Derek finally pulled up to the front doors of the ER, she glanced over. "I should be finished by seven-thirty, but I'll call if I'm running late."

"Sounds good. See you then."

She climbed out of the car and waved goodbye. As she walked inside, she told herself there was no reason to worry about Derek and Lexi leaving town. Not today and certainly not on the Fourth of July holiday. After all, Derek was planning on taking Lexi to the parade.

So why did she have this nagging sense of impending doom?

She shrugged off the feeling and did her best to concentrate on the patients that were located on her team for the day. The hospital census was high, which unfortunately meant long wait times for patients who needed to be admitted. One thing she liked about working in the ER was that there was always a wide variety of patients—from minor injuries from burns, heatstroke, and alcohol intoxication to more serious injuries from a four-car motor vehicle crash on the interstate.

Her brother called several more times without leaving a message, so she called him back on her lunch break. He didn't answer, so she left him a message, explaining she was at work and she'd try to call him when she was finished. Guiltily, she remembered she hadn't called him last night, either.

She hoped Zack was doing all right and found herself worrying about her brother as her afternoon wore on. Zack had been in a rough place for a long time, but no matter how much she begged him, he'd refused to return to Crystal Lake.

Or to church.

Despite the high level of activity, her shift dragged on for what seemed like forever. There was a brief lull around dinnertime, which gave her hope that she'd actually get out on time.

She called Derek's mobile phone, relieved when he answered on the first ring. "Hi, how was the parade?"

"Great." His voice sounded strained. "What time do you want me to pick you up?"

"I should get out of here on time, so seven-thirty is fine. Is something wrong?"

"No, nothing's wrong. I cooked the pork chops you had in the freezer for dinner. Hope that's okay."

"Sure, that's fine." All her instincts were on alert. She couldn't shake the feeling that something bad had rattled Derek. Since she didn't really have time to talk, she didn't push the issue. "See you soon."

"Sounds good." Derek hung up before she could say anything more.

She punched out at seven-thirty, and as she walked outside to meet Derek, her brother called again. "Where have you been?" Zack demanded. "I've been trying to get a hold of you for the past two days."

"I was working. Why? What's going on?"

"We need to talk. Is that Ryerson guy still staying with you?"

"Yes, Zack, I already told you he was planning to stay through the holiday. Why?"

"I was running a search on him and discovered St. Louis has a court order out against him. He's bad news, Jules. You need to kick him out right away."

Derek drove up in her car, his expression looking grim. And she knew that her brother had interfered in Derek's personal business. "Where are you, Zack? Did you drive up here to talk to Derek?"

"Maybe I did drive up to serve the court order. So what? Just because he plans to slap up some drywall doesn't mean he can use you as a shield against a custody suit. He has seventy-two hours to bring his daughter back to St. Louis or they'll put out a warrant for his arrest."

"Look, I'll talk to Derek, okay? I have to go. I'll call you back in a little while." Her mind was racing as she disconnected from the call.

Derek's car accident was on Friday evening, and it must have been sometime after the weekend that Lexi's grandparents had gone to court to file the order demanding Derek bring Lexi back to St. Louis.

Yesterday was Monday, and frankly, she was surprised the court order had gone in so quickly. And equally shocked that the Hope County Sheriff's Department hadn't known about it yesterday when Derek had applied for the dispatch job.

Although maybe they wouldn't know until the seventy-two-hour timeframe had passed and the arrest warrant was issued. Her brother's butting into her business gave them the advance notice they needed.

She walked over to the car. "There's something you need to know," he said.

"I already heard from Zack," she interrupted. "I'm sorry he stuck his nose into your business, but don't you see? This is actually good news."

Derek's scowl deepened. "You're kidding, right?"

"No, just listen to me for a minute," she said. "At least you were given the court order right away, so there's plenty of time for us to take action."

"Take action?" he glanced over at her as he navigated the traffic around town. "Look, Julie, I appreciate everything you did for me and Lexi, but we need to hit the road. The sooner the better."

Hit the road? Was he crazy? "Derek, there's no point in running again. Don't you see? It's just a matter of time before the police find you. And by then, your reputation will be shot, which will only give Lexi's grandparents the upper hand."

"What choice do I have?" he asked.

She gave him an exasperated look. "You can go back to St. Louis and face Claire's parents. You can convince them to drop this ridiculous notion of fighting for custody."

12

"Going back to St. Louis is not an option," Derek said harshly. He gripped the steering wheel so hard his knuckles went white, and he had to bite back a flash of anger. Julie had no idea what she was talking about. Why had he thought she would take his side? Hadn't he known all along that her Christian conscience would force her into turning him over to the authorities?

If he was hurt by her unwillingness to go along with his plan, he had no one to blame but himself.

"Why is running away a better option?" she demanded.

"Keeping Lexi safe is the only option." He wasn't going to waste time arguing. Besides, he'd already heard all this and more from her brother, Zack, when he'd slapped the court order into his hand. He'd immediately jumped into action. His and Lexi's suitcases were packed and ready to go. He'd have already left town except for the fact that he hadn't been able to get in touch with Henry to snag one of his cheap rental cars. For some reason, he hadn't expected the old guy to close up on the holiday.

"Derek," she started, but he cut him off with a stern look.

"Not now." They'd already said far too much in front of Lexi. Glancing in the rearview mirror, he wasn't surprised to see Lexi rocking back and forth in her booster seat, a sure sign of distress. "How are you doing back there, baby-doll? Are you okay?" he asked in a cheerful tone.

Lexi didn't answer, and he battled another wave of helpless frustration. Why couldn't Claire's parents leave him alone? Lexi had been doing so well over the past few days. She'd even brought up her mother to Julie. He didn't like the thought of Lexi regressing back to her protective wall of silence, which he knew would happen once they left town.

He glanced over at Julie, who was staring straight ahead, her lips pressed together in a firm line. She wouldn't talk any more in front of Lexi, but he knew she didn't consider their discussion finished.

But it didn't matter what arguments she was likely formulating in her mind. She didn't know Claire's parents. Didn't have any idea what he was up against. What chance did an unemployed soldier have against a wealthy couple?

None whatsoever.

When he pulled into Julie's driveway, he was relieved to see that Zack's squad car was gone. Not that it really mattered, since the damage was done.

"Derek, be reasonable," Julie pleaded in a low tone after Lexi ran inside.

He raised his eyebrows in disbelief. "Me? You want me to be reasonable? Didn't you hear a word I told you last night about Claire's parents? They have judges on their side. What do I have? Nothing. Claire wasn't even my wife." He could barely hold back his frustration. The situation couldn't get much worse. He didn't even have enough money for a decent lawyer.

"We have God on our side, Derek," Julie said softly.

"We? You're not involved in this mess; it's just me and Lexi. I don't need your help or God's help, either. Excuse me," he muttered as he brushed past her to head inside.

He didn't see Lexi inside and knew she was probably hiding in the bedroom. For a moment, he stood there and stared at the packed suitcases he'd left standing in the center of the room. He really needed Henry to call him back because he wasn't going to get very far without a ride. And considering their recent argument, he didn't think Julie would be willing to drive him to the bus station in Madison.

He let out a heavy sigh as he scrubbed his hands over his face. Just a few hours ago, he'd been so full of hope that things were finally going in the right direction. He'd finished tearing down the drywall off the ceiling, leaving the bare studs ready to be covered with new Sheetrock. He felt a stab of remorse that he wouldn't be able to finish the job.

Small payment for everything Julie had done for him. He suspected she'd keep on giving if he let her, but enough was enough. He and Lexi would figure something out. They'd be fine.

But he couldn't deny he'd miss Crystal Lake once he was gone. And Julie.

Especially Julie.

"Lexi?" Derek called as he walked down the hall toward the bedroom. He looked in the bathroom and both bedrooms, but Lexi was nowhere to be found.

Panic tightened his chest. Where was she? With Julie?

Derek strode outside and rapped lightly on the wood frame of Julie's patio door. "Julie? Is Lexi with you?"

Julie came over to meet him, a tiny frown furrowed in her brow. "No, Lexi isn't with me. I thought she was with you. She went into your side of the townhouse, didn't she?"

"Yes, but I can't find her. She might be hiding. Can we look around your place?"

"Of course." She opened the screen door and let him in.

Between the two of them, it didn't take long to validate the townhouse was empty. His stomach knotted with anxiety as he went back outside onto the patio. "Lexi!" he shouted. "Come home right now!"

"You don't think she went down to the lake by herself, do you?" Julie asked. She came outside still wearing her scrubs from work. "Maybe we should check the boat."

Derek was already jogging down toward the lakefront. "Lexi!" Sheer desperation laced his tone. "She's never done anything like this," he muttered.

Julie swallowed hard. "We shouldn't have said anything in front of her," she said softly.

"She was upset before I picked you up," he said, knowing full well this mess was his fault. "Your brother and I argued a bit, and then when I packed our suitcases, I could tell Lexi was distressed." Derek jumped onto the boat. "Lexi?" He looked around at all the places a six-year-old might use to hide, not that there were many.

But the boat was empty.

An overwhelming sense of helplessness hit hard. Where was his daughter?

Dear Lord, help me! Please help me find Lexi! Please keep her safe from harm!

JULIE FOLLOWED Derek down to the boat, raking her gaze over the lake to be sure the little girl hadn't fallen in the water. "Lexi!" she shouted, adding her voice to Derek's.

"Dear Lord, help me find her," Derek murmured as he jumped off the boat back on land.

She grasped his hand and held on tightly. "God will help us find her, Derek. She couldn't have gone far."

He squeezed her hand. "Let's split up. You check the front, and I'll keep looking here in the back."

"All right." She hurried back up to the house, making a sweep around Derek's side in case the little girl was crouched somewhere over there. But there was no sign of Lexi, even when she went around to the front. "Lexi!" she yelled, heading out to the street. The sun was low on the horizon, and it wouldn't take long for darkness to fall. They needed to find Lexi and fast.

Could she have walked down the road? Julie debated taking the car and driving around the area but didn't want to leave without telling Derek.

She darted inside the house to grab her car keys but then remembered Derek had been the one to drive home. She went back outside to find him. "Do you have my keys? I thought I'd take the car and look for her."

"Sure." He tugged the keys from his pocket. "Wait a minute, did you check the garden?"

"No." She followed Derek over to the far right side of the townhouse where her small garden was located. Relief whooshed out when she saw Lexi huddled between the house and the garden, rocking back and forth.

"Lexi, honey, you scared me," Derek said as he walked

over to crouch down beside his daughter. "Didn't you hear me calling you?"

"Don't want to go, don't want to go, don't want to go," Lexi repeated over and over again.

Julie's heart went out to the little girl as Derek gathered her into his arms and rose to his feet. She couldn't hear what he murmured, but the way he clutched her close, she knew he was trying to reassure her.

"Is there anything I can do?" she asked softly.

"Not really." Derek didn't show any signs of discomfort from his ribs as he carried Lexi back toward his side of the townhouse. "I guess we'll spend the night here, if that's okay with you."

"Of course it's okay," she responded. "It's too late to do anything more tonight, anyway."

"Thanks." He gave her a brief nod before disappearing inside.

Julie walked into her kitchen more slowly, wishing there was some way to convince Derek to face Lexi's grandparents. She understood that they were prominent members of the community, but surely a biological father had rights, too? She'd be more than happy to testify on his behalf if needed. Maybe she was being overly optimistic about his chances, but certainly he needed to try. Why couldn't he see that running away would only make things worse?

She went into the bathroom to wash up and then changed into a pair of comfy sweats, considering the air outside had turned a bit cool. She was too distracted to sleep, however, so she went back into the kitchen to make a cup of herbal tea to help her relax.

The plate of grilled pork chops and green beans Derek had thoughtfully left for her was still on the counter, but she wasn't a bit hungry. Just the thought of food made her stomach roll with nausea.

A shadow outside on the patio caught her eye. She froze but then relaxed when she realized Derek was sitting outside in the darkness, holding his head in his hands.

She told herself not to go outside, that Derek needed to work this through on his own. But her silent lecture didn't do any good. In less than two minutes, she found herself quietly sliding open the patio door and stepping outside.

He didn't look up when she approached, either, because he hadn't heard her or because he wanted to be alone.

Yet she couldn't just leave him out here. "Hey. Are you okay?" she asked, dropping into a chair beside him.

He lifted his head, but she couldn't read his expression in the darkness. "I've never been so scared," he murmured. "If anything had happened to her, I would have never forgiven myself."

"I know." She ached to comfort him. "But Lexi's okay."

"She's not okay," Derek muttered. "This has been rough on her."

There wasn't much she could say to that. "I'm sorry," she said helplessly.

He shook his head. "I've been sitting here praying for guidance, but so far the only answer seems to be to do what you suggested—go back to St. Louis and face Claire's parents."

Her heart filled with hope. "God knows what's best."

"I'm surprised He's listening to me," Derek confessed softly. "After everything that happened with Claire and the Afghani soldiers I've killed..." His voice trailed off.

"Derek, God is always there for us, especially during those times we need Him the most." She could only imagine what horrors he'd lived through in Afghanistan, and she understood a little better why he'd resisted going to church. "God would never turn against you. But maybe you gave up on Him?"

He let out a heavy sigh. "Maybe. It's hard to hang on to faith when you're watching your men dying around you. The Bible teaches us to turn the other cheek, but instead we're sent out there to kill the enemy. There were times I looked down at my hands and could only see the blood of the lives I'd taken."

She put her arm around his shoulders and gave him a hug. "Derek, I'm sorry you had to go through all that. But you need to know, God is still there for you. All you have to do is believe."

"You've helped remind me about that," he admitted. "I guess I've been lost for a while now."

"Or maybe you weren't lost at all. It could be that God intended for you to come here all along," she pointed out. "God often takes matters into His own hands."

The moonlight revealed a ghost of a smile. "You could be right about that."

She gave him another quick hug. "So does this mean you're going to head back to St. Louis?"

The smile faded. "Yes, but I don't know if facing Claire's parents will do any good." He abruptly pulled away and rose to his feet, pacing the small length of the patio. "What if I lose Lexi? I can't imagine a life without my daughter. She's all I have left in the world."

"They can't take her completely away," she reasoned, trying to use logic to cut through his fear. "You would still have some rights."

He let out a harsh sound. "What, visits every other weekend? While she struggles in that ridiculous school they forced on her? No, I can't do that. I won't do that."

She understood his angst. What Claire's parents were doing was so wrong, there just had to be a way to get through to them. "What can I do to help?" she asked. "There has to be a way to ensure that you don't lose custody of your daughter."

"I wish I knew," he said with a heavy sigh. He tipped his head back to gaze up at the stars. "I know I need to leave this in God's hands, but it isn't easy. She's my whole life."

There was a tiny part of her that wished she was part of his life, too. But of course, his daughter had to come first. "I'd like to come with you," she offered tentatively. She rose to walk over to his side. "You don't have to do this alone. Maybe I can help make Claire's parents see what a great father you've been. I'd even testify in court if necessary."

He went still, looking down at her. She wished she could see the expression in his eyes. "Julie, you've already given us so much, I can't possibly accept anything more. It's not right for me to take advantage of you."

"That's Zack talking," she said with a scowl. "I bet he's the one who said that to you, right?"

Derek shrugged, which was answer enough.

"Why can't you believe that I care about you and Lexi?" she asked. "I can't stand the thought of the court system tearing you apart."

"I don't deserve someone like you," he murmured. And when he reached out to draw her close, she didn't resist but went willingly into his arms.

He tipped her face up to kiss her, and she reveled in the gentle sweep of his mouth against hers. Their first kiss had been an accident, but this time, she knew he meant to kiss her.

And she absolutely meant to kiss him back.

All too soon, he broke off the kiss, tilting his head back

and taking several deep breaths, and she smiled when she felt the racing beat of his heart. "I think it's time for me to go," he said huskily.

She buried her face against his chest, holding on to him for a moment longer, wishing she didn't have to let go. But since they couldn't stand here like this all night, she forced herself to take a step back. "All right," she agreed reluctantly, trying to smile. "But you didn't answer my question."

"What question?" he asked wryly. "Apparently, my mind turns to mush around you."

She had to laugh. "About whether or not you'll let me come with you to St. Louis. I'm off tomorrow and can probably switch shifts for Thursday, too. If you'd like some moral support."

He was quiet for so long she thought he was going to insist on going alone. "I'd like that," he finally said softly. "If you're absolutely sure about going along."

"I'm sure." She hoped her relief wasn't too evident. "Goodnight, Derek."

"Goodnight, Julie."

She went inside to get ready for bed, thinking that she was already far too emotionally involved with Derek and Lexi.

What if he did succeed in maintaining custody of his daughter? He might decide to stay in St. Louis to be near Lexi's grandparents. They might even work out some sort of arrangement where Lexi would stay with her grandparents before and after school, which would help Derek out when he found a job.

She didn't have a right to be sad, but she couldn't ignore the distinct impression that helping Derek would only take him and Lexi away from her forever.

Leaving her alone again.

13

Derek negotiated the heavy traffic of St. Louis with dread curling in his stomach. The entire trip had been far from smooth—getting Lexi to agree to get in the car at all had been a major feat in and of itself. She'd only given in when Julie agreed to sit in the backseat with her.

Now that they were close to their destination, tempers were running a big ragged. In the cold light of day, he was second-guessing his decision. He wasn't even sure what he was going to say to Claire's parents. Hi, how are you, and how dare you try to take my daughter away from me? Yeah, somehow he didn't think that line was going to work well for him.

"Maybe this wasn't a good idea," he murmured in a low voice, glancing over at Julie seated in the passenger seat. Once they'd stopped for lunch, Lexi had been a little better about letting Julie sit up front with him. "I'm worried about how Claire's parents are going to react to all of us showing up unannounced on their doorstep."

Julie reached over and gave his hand a small squeeze.

"We can only control our own reactions, not theirs. All we can do is be nice and respectful. At the very least, they'll know that you're not giving up easily. Better to know what you're facing now than to be blindsided in front of the judge."

He knew she was right and tried to relax his death grip on the steering wheel. St. Louis had its usual snarl of traffic, but thankfully, Lexi's grandparents lived in one of the ritzy suburbs outside of the city, so he was able to exit off the interstate and get out of the traffic without having to go through the maze of downtown St. Louis.

Despite how he'd tried to rehearse what he was going to say, his mind went blank when he finally pulled into their driveway in front of the massive three-car garage. The mansion where Claire had grown up loomed large and intimidating, and he had to force himself to park Julie's car and turn off the engine. Any hope that they might not be home fled when the front door opened, revealing the distinguished figure of Claire's father, Robert Donnell.

Derek shoved open his door at the same time Julie slid out of the passenger seat. Julie opened the back passenger door for Lexi, who climbed down, obviously eager to get out of the constraints of her booster seat.

"Lexi!" Claire's father called out from the front porch. "Come give your grandpa a hug!"

"Hi, Grandpa," Lexi called but instead of running over to greet him, she clung to Julie's hand.

For a moment, he thought he saw a flash of pain cross the older man's features and felt a surge of sympathy. Derek hastily came around the car and put his hand against Julie's back, gently leading her forward. "Mr. Donnell, I'd like you to meet Julie Crain. Julie, this is Lexi's grandfather, Mr. Robert Donnell."

"It's so nice to meet you, Mr. Donnell," Julie said, approaching the house with Lexi trailing along by her side. "Derek has told me so much about you."

Robert scowled at her, but Julie's smile never wavered. He had the wild idea that Julie intended to smother the old guy with kindness until he gave in and dropped the custody suit. Julie held out her hand, forcing Mr. Donnell to take it in a brief handshake before he turned his attention to his granddaughter. "Lexi, we've missed you so much," he said, reaching for her.

Lexi shrank back against Julie as if she didn't have good memories of being with her grandparents. "Can we go home now?" she asked. "I want to go for a boat ride."

Robert's eyes narrowed with anger. "You've turned my granddaughter against me," he accused.

"No, of course not. Lexi's just tired after the long car ride, right, Lexi?" Julie gave his daughter's shoulders a brief squeeze. "Lexi, it's not nice to be rude," she chided gently.

Derek took charge of the deteriorating situation. "Look, Mr. Donnell, I'm sorry to show up uninvited, but we just want a chance to discuss things with you and Mrs. Donnell. Why don't we sit down for a few minutes? Wouldn't it be better to talk now than having this conversation in front of the judge?"

"Hrumph," the older man grunted but reluctantly opened the door for them. "Gladys?" he called back over his shoulder. "Derek brought Lexi back along with his new girl-friend." There was no mistaking the snide tone in his voice as they stepped into the cool interior of the house.

He caught sight of Julie's wince and wondered if she resented being referred to as his girlfriend. The idea both-ered him, considering he rather liked the label. Their heated kiss has cost him a good night's sleep, but maybe she regretted the moment of intimacy? Too bad they hadn't had a chance to talk alone before hitting the road. They certainly hadn't discussed anything in front of Lexi.

Shaking off his disturbing thoughts, he followed Robert into the formal living room. The one where he always felt as if he had to be extra careful or he might accidently break something.

Claire's mother hurried in, looking drawn and worried despite her blindingly white linen pants and ruffled blue blouse. She was always dressed to perfection, and today was no different. "Lexi!" she gushed. "Oh, sweetie, we've missed you so much!"

Derek had to bite his tongue to prevent himself from pointing out they'd only been gone five days, not five months. But he held his silence as Lexi tolerated a brief hug from her grandmother before wiggling away.

"Mrs. Donnell, this is Julie Crain. She's an ER nurse working at the Hope County Hospital," he said, introducing Julie. "Julie, this is Lexi's grandmother, Mrs. Donnell."

"It's nice to meet you," Julie said warmly. "You have a beautiful home."

Mrs. Donnell pursed her lips together in a disapproving frown. "I'm sorry we're forced to meet under these circumstances," she said primly. She turned toward her granddaughter. "Lexi, how would you like to play with your dollhouse up in your room?"

Lexi silently shook her head, and Derek swallowed a sigh. Lexi didn't play with dolls, at least not that he'd ever noted. But clearly, Claire's parents wanted her to.

"Actually, she'd probably love to draw a picture for us," Derek said. "Would you like to run and get your sketchbook?" he asked his daughter. "I'm sure Grandma and

Grandpa would love a pretty picture from their grand-daughter."

Lexi's eyes brightened, and she nodded eagerly.

"I'll take her out for the sketchbook," Julie offered.

"Thanks," he murmured, even though he would have liked to have Julie stay right beside him for moral support. But he didn't blame her for wanting to escape, considering the hostile atmosphere they'd stepped into. The entire scene was going worse than he'd anticipated.

Julie gave him a bracing smile as she took Lexi back outside.

But she'd barely cleared the doorway when Claire's mother made a low, hissing sound. "How dare you bring that woman into our home!"

Derek didn't appreciate the vicious attack on Julie but tried to hold back his temper. "This isn't about Julie, who has been nothing but kind to me and Lexi, so please keep her out of this."

"You claimed you loved Claire," Robert accused, siding with his wife. "But it sure didn't take you long to move on to someone else, now did it?"

He'd remained standing, facing them both and feeling seriously outnumbered. "There's no need to jump to conclusions. Julie is not my girlfriend, but she is a good friend and doesn't deserve your anger. Why on earth are you upset?" he asked, truly confused. "You know very well you didn't want Claire to marry me. I did care about Claire very much, and you know we both loved Lexi. And Lexi is the reason I'm here. I need you to help me understand why you're so determined to take my daughter away from me."

Gladys and Robert exchanged a somber look. "I'm sorry that you feel this way, but we think Lexi is better off with us," Robert said. "She needs the financial security we can offer."

Financial security? It was all he could do not to scoff at their idea of what Lexi needed. "Money doesn't automatically bring happiness. Lexi needs love and understanding more than she needs your financial security." He tried to think of a way to get through to them. "Did you ever ask yourselves why Claire ran off to the Fort Drum Army Base in the first place?" he asked. He wasn't sure how much they knew about the time he and Claire first met. "She told me she couldn't relax and just be herself around you."

"You dare speak to us like that about our own daughter?" Gladys demanded, her beautiful face, so much like Claire's, was twisted with anger. "Claire loved us and proved that by coming home to us after you left her pregnant and alone."

He hadn't left Claire pregnant and alone, he'd asked her to marry him, and she'd refused. But he knew that no matter what he said, there was no way to win Claire's parents over. Hadn't he already tried that over the past six years since Lexi was born? They refused to believe anything that didn't fit into their idea of a perfect little world. He remembered Julie's comment about how he could only control his reactions, not theirs.

"Yes, Claire loved you both very much, and I don't want to fight with you. I just want you to understand that I love Lexi. I'm her father, and she needs me, just as much as she needs the both of you. Together, we can be a complete family for Lexi, but not if you insist on tearing us apart."

They didn't say anything, and while their stern expressions didn't give much away, he sensed he might be getting through to them. At least a little. "I think that's what Claire would want," he added. "Don't you?"

JULIE TOOK her time digging Lexi's sketchbook out of the trunk of her car. As much as she would have preferred to stay outside, the sun was beating down mercilessly as it was far hotter here than in Crystal Lake, Wisconsin. Within five minutes, she was sweating profusely, so she took Lexi back into the house, slipping past the three adults standing in the formal living room to make her way into the kitchen. The least she could do was give Derek and Claire's parents some privacy.

It pained her to admit that he'd been right about them. She'd never met two more miserable people. She understood they were grieving over the loss of their daughter, and truly, their hostility toward her wasn't what made her upset. It was the way they treated Lexi. Dolls? Really? They didn't know the first thing about the granddaughter they claimed to love.

Derek's assessment had been dead-on. Lexi's grandparents seemed intent on forcing the child to fit into the mold of a "perfect granddaughter."

But why couldn't they accept that Lexi was perfect just the way she was?

She sighed and shook her head. She'd sincerely believed the judge would grant custody to Derek, but now she wasn't so sure.

"Do you think my picture will make Grandma and Grandpa happy again?" Lexi asked as she worked on her drawing.

Julie was amazed at how astute Lexi was, picking up on

the underlying anger radiating from her grandparents. "I sure hope so, sweetie," she said.

Movement from the corner of her eye had her straightening in her chair. "Hi, Mrs. Donnell," she greeted the woman hovering in the doorway. "I hope you don't mind that we made ourselves at home in your kitchen. Lexi prefers to draw while sitting at a table."

The older woman gave a brief nod. "Derek tells me you're not his girlfriend."

Keeping her smile in place took considerable effort. "I consider Derek a very good friend. He's a great guy and a wonderful father. I've enjoyed getting to know him. And of course, Lexi." She gestured to Lexi's picture. "Have you seen the talent she has? I told Derek she should be in some sort of art program."

Mrs. Donnell took a step closer to peer at Lexi's drawing. "She does a very nice job," she agreed.

Nice? The woman was clueless. "I had a niece, Amelia, who was about Lexi's age before she died of leukemia. Amelia was a wonderful little girl, loved dolls and playing make-believe, but she couldn't draw anything more than stick-people. Each child has her own individual talents. Amelia's was to make people smile. Maybe Lexi's is to touch people through her art."

"I'm almost finished, Grandma," Lexi said. She made a few more strokes with her pencil before lifting up the picture and handing it to her grandmother. "See? I made a picture of Mommy. She's an angel up in heaven with God. Julie says she's up there right now, watching over me."

"Oh," Gladys whispered, her eyes brimming with tears as she gazed down at Lexi's angel, who had feather-light wings and wore a gentle smile. "That's a beautiful picture, Lexi. Thank you so much."

"Don't be sad. Mommy is watching over you and Grandpa, too," Lexi said. "Right Julie?"

She had to fight her own tears in order to answer. "Yes, that's exactly right, Lexi. Remember, we are never alone, for God is always with us."

"I...excuse me," Gladys rushed out of the room, clutching Lexi's picture to her chest.

"I wanted her to be happy," Lexi said with a frown.

"Don't worry, Lexi," she murmured, giving Lexi a brief hug. At that moment, Julie realized that Lexi's grandparents weren't trying to change Lexi into the perfect granddaughter.

They wanted Lexi to be just like Claire. Because they wanted their daughter back.

Poor, misguided souls. "Your picture was perfect and exactly what your grandmother needed."

Lexi seemed to consider this for a moment. "Okay, so now can we go home?"

"Soon," she murmured. "Hopefully we can go home soon, Lexi."

———————

DEREK TUGGED at the neckline of his starched shirt, waiting for the judge to enter the chambers. Lexi was seated beside him, looking very pretty in a blue dress that matched the color of her eyes. Julie sat behind them as they waited for Claire's parents to show up.

With barely five minutes to spare, the doors of the courtroom opened, revealing Robert and Gladys Donnell and their lawyer. They sat down at the table next to him, looking impressive dressed in their formal clothing.

"Hi, Grandma; hi, Grandpa," Lexi said in a loud whisper.

The older couple looked distinctly uncomfortable as they glanced over at him and Lexi. He couldn't afford a lawyer and had refused Julie's offer to pay for one. He wasn't sure how a lawyer would help, anyway; if he couldn't convince the judge on his own, then he was in deep trouble.

Lexi moved closer, and he put his arm around her tiny shoulders. "This will all be over soon, baby-doll," he murmured.

"Then we can go home?" Lexi asked. "I really, really want to go for a boat ride."

He smothered a smile when Robert and Gladys frowned darkly. He knew it bothered them that Lexi kept asking to go home, as in back to Crystal Lake.

"All rise," the deputy said. "The honorable Judge Berkley presiding."

Since he and Lexi were already standing, he simply straightened his spine and focused on the judge. A sharp stab of panic dug deep when the judge nodded at the Donnells as if he knew them.

"Please be seated," Judge Berkley said.

Derek reluctantly sat down, drawing Lexi into the chair beside him.

"This is a preliminary hearing to determine whether or not custody of the minor, known as Alexis Claire, should be removed from her biological father, Derek Ryerson, and granted in turn to her grandparents, Robert and Gladys Donnell."

"Excuse me, your honor, but may I ask on what grounds?" Derek asked.

The judge tipped his head down to peer at Derek over

the rims of his glasses. "Based on what's best for Alexus, that's what grounds."

Derek was determined not to lose his temper. "Yes, Your Honor, I believe we all want what is best for Lexi. But I still don't understand why my custodial rights are being challenged. I love my daughter, and she loves me. I have never hurt her or failed to provide for her needs. She's been through a very difficult time after losing her mother. The last thing she needs is to lose her father as well. So again, Your Honor, I ask on what grounds is this matter being heard?"

"Your Honor, I would like to make a statement," Robert Donnell said as he rose to his feet. "We asked for this hearing because Derek Ryerson has removed our granddaughter from the private school we'd placed her in. A private school that can offer her more structure and more learning than the public school system. And we feel that Derek Ryerson was not acting in his daughter's best interests when he removed her from this highly regarded academic program."

Judge Berkley sat back in his seat and looked back at Derek. "Is Mr. Donnell's statement true?"

Derek forced a smile. "Your Honor, Lexi cried every morning that she was forced to go to that school. I fail to see how sending her there is acting in her best interest."

"That's not true," Robert said swiftly. He turned to face Derek. "You're just saying that."

"Stop it!" Mrs. Donnell's voice rang through the courtroom. "This is wrong, Robert. We shouldn't be tearing this family apart. We should be trying to hold it together."

Derek stared in shock at Claire's mother. He'd never in his wildest dreams imagined the woman would unbend enough to come to his defense. All along, he'd been banking on wearing Robert down.

"Gladys," Robert protested.

"No, will you please just listen to me for once? What we're doing is wrong. It's not going to bring Claire back." Gladys glanced over at Derek, a naked plea in her gaze. "Derek, if we drop this custody matter, will you please allow us to see Lexi on a regular basis? All we really want is to be a part of our granddaughter's life. Please?"

"Of course I'll let you see Lexi," he said slowly, his mind reeling from the turn of events. "I never intended to keep her away from you. She needs her grandparents." He didn't add that he'd only left town in the first place because they'd threatened to take Lexi away from him.

"All right, then it's settled." Apparently, Gladys had made up her mind. "See, Robert? Everything is going to be just fine."

Robert glanced over at Derek and Lexi, as if he wasn't quite ready to give in. But then Lexi smiled at him. "I love you, Grandpa," she said.

The older man crumpled. "I love you, too, Lexi." Derek gave his daughter a nudge, and she ran over to give her grandparents a hug.

Relieved, he glanced back at Julie, not the least bit surprised to see big, silent tears rolling down her cheeks. "I knew God would take care of you," she whispered.

"I know," he whispered back. The weight he'd been carrying for the past few weeks finally rolled off his shoulders, leaving him lightheaded with relief.

His nightmare was finally over.

14

J ulie smiled so much she thought her face might crack and crumble into tiny pieces. As they stood on the steps of the courthouse, she listened as Gladys talked about enrolling Lexi in an art program and enthusiastically made plans for a cookout over the upcoming weekend. Even Robert had softened toward Derek, and she wondered if the original job offer he'd taken from Derek would be reinstated.

Things were working out exactly the way they were supposed to. She was so happy for Derek.

And so sad for herself.

She slipped away from the crowd, intending to head back to her car to begin the long ride home, when Derek's hand on her arm stopped her. "Hey, where are you going?"

She closed her eyes and mentally braced herself to turn and face him. "I need to head home, Derek. It's a long drive, and I have to work tomorrow."

"The Donnells want to take us out for brunch."

"I think that's a great idea. I'm sure being together as a family will do wonders for Lexi."

His intense blue gaze searched hers. "Why don't you join us?" he asked softly.

Her heart squeezed, and she had to swallow the lump in her throat. "I think it's best if I head home," she said. "Dropping the custody battle is a big step for the Donnells, and I think the four of you could use a little bonding time together."

Without her being the unintended painful reminder that Claire wasn't here anymore.

A hint of uncertainty flashed in his eyes, but after a long moment, he nodded. "I think you might be right," he agreed. "Thanks for everything, Julie."

He drew her in for a hug, and she clung to him for a moment before gathering the strength to pull away. "Take care, Derek."

"Wait." He caught her hand before she could leave. "Aren't you going to say goodbye to Lexi?"

Her heart was breaking, but of course she couldn't leave without saying goodbye to Lexi. When Derek called his daughter's name, she came running over.

"I'm hungry, Daddy. Grandma says we're going for blunch."

"Brunch," he corrected softly, running a hand over his daughter's glossy, dark hair. "Breakfast and lunch together is brunch."

Julie smiled down at Lexi and forced a cheerfulness she was far from feeling into her tone. "Have fun. Unfortunately, I have to head home, Lexi." She wrapped her arm around the child's shoulders. "Goodbye, sweetie. Take good care of your daddy, okay?"

"Do you hafta go?" Lexi asked, returning her hug and staring up at her with a plaintive gaze that reminded her too much of Derek. "I want you to stay."

She wanted to stay, too, but she understood that staying here wasn't part of God's plan. "I'm afraid so, sweetie. I have to work at the hospital again very soon." Her vision went blurry, and she had to sniffle back her tears. "I love you, Lexi," she said huskily. She released the child and turned to walk away, hardly able to see where she was going.

It took every bit of strength she possessed not to turn and look back at what she was leaving behind.

———————

JULIE REPORTED for her shift at seven a.m. the following morning, hoping no one would notice the puffiness of her eyes from her crying jag the night before.

But, of course, she couldn't fool her friend Merry. "What happened?" she demanded. "Did he hurt you?"

"Nothing happened." Julie couldn't have pasted a smile on her face if her life depended on it. "Derek went back home to his family, that's all."

"Oh, Jules," Merry said, giving her a quick hug. "I'm sorry."

"Don't be, it's certainly not your fault. And you did warn me, remember?" She pulled away from her friend to glance up at the patient board, desperately needing the distraction of work. "Fill me in on my patients, okay?"

She sensed Merry wanted to say more, but her pager went off, announcing the arrival of an ambulance. "I've assigned you to team three today," Merry said. "Ask Debra to give you the rundown while I go check on this new arrival, okay?"

"Sure," she murmured as Merry hurried away.

The shift started out busy, but around lunchtime, there was a definite lull, giving her far too much time to think. To wonder what Derek and Lexi were doing. To wonder if they missed her just a fraction of how much she missed them.

To wonder if she should try inviting them up for a weekend sometime soon for a picnic and boat ride on the lake.

No, don't even think about it, she told herself sternly. Derek and Lexi were back in St. Louis where they belonged. No point in dragging the agony out even further. She was happy for them and for the Donnells, who would still get to see their granddaughter.

The time she'd had here with Derek and Lexi had just been a tiny detour for them. And she had no one to blame but herself for getting too emotionally involved.

By the time her twelve-hour shift was over at seven-thirty in the evening, she was battling a wave of over-whelming exhaustion. Lack of sleep from the night before hadn't helped. She dragged herself out to her car and headed home.

When she pulled into the driveway, she heard the faint sound of laughter coming from the back side of the town-house and inwardly groaned. Obviously, the tourists were still playing out on the lake while she wanted nothing more than to crawl into bed, pull the sheet over her head to shut out the rest of the world, and try to get some sleep.

Which wasn't likely unless Derek and Lexi stopped invading her dreams.

As she climbed out of the car, she heard the front door slam. Alarmed, she whirled around and dropped her jaw when she saw Derek and Lexi walking over the front lawn toward her. Belatedly, she recognized a strange car parked along the opposite side of the street.

"Hi, Julie." Lexi greeted her with an enthusiastic hug.

"Hi, Lexi, Derek." She returned Lexi's hug but couldn't tear her gaze away from Derek. "What are you doing here?" she sputtered.

He lifted a brow. "I did a little work on the townhouse, and then Lexi and I made dinner. Hope you're hungry?"

She knew she was gaping but couldn't seem to pull herself together. "But how? Why?"

He chuckled, and she realized that, in all the time they spent together, she'd rarely heard Derek laugh. "I borrowed a car from Claire's parents and you don't lock your doors in Crystal Lake, remember?"

That wasn't what she meant, but she was so thrilled to see them she didn't care. "I'm just surprised to see you, that's all," she managed. "I wasn't expecting this."

"It's great to see you, too," he said in a low, husky tone. For a moment, his gaze bored into hers, but then he smiled and reached for her hand. "Come on, I want to show you what I managed to get done today," he said, tugging her toward the townhouse.

She didn't understand how he'd gotten anything done, considering it was a long drive up from St. Louis, but when he opened the front door with a flourish, she realized he'd completed one entire wall with new drywall. "Derek! This looks amazing!" Then she scowled. "You did this with your sore ribs, didn't you?" she demanded.

"I'm fine," he assured her, grinning from ear to ear. "But it looks great, doesn't it? If I do say so myself," he added modestly.

She shot him an exasperated grin. "Yes, it does."

"Come on, let's eat. I have some marinated chicken breasts on the grill, and hope you don't mind, but Lexi and I helped ourselves to your garden to put together a salad."

"Of course I don't mind," she said. How could she when she was still reeling from the knowledge that Derek had come back? To see her?

Or maybe just to repay a debt. As she followed Derek outside to the patio, she glanced back one more time at the finished wall and told herself not to get too excited about his being there. Now that she really thought about it, she figured he'd only returned to finish his part of the deal. Not that she'd expected anything more from him, but she sensed his pride wouldn't allow him to leave the job undone.

And if that was the case, she had no idea how she'd manage to protect her heart long enough for him to finish the stupid townhouse.

———

Derek found it increasingly difficult to keep his gaze off Julie as they ate the meal he'd prepared. The moment she'd arrived home, he'd wanted nothing more than to sweep her into his arms and kiss her soundly but had held back for two reasons. First of all, because she'd left St. Louis so abruptly, which made him wonder how she felt about him and secondly, because he knew Lexi was watching.

Hopefully, Lexi would be tired from their trip and go to bed sooner than later. He wanted, needed a little time alone with Julie.

As soon as they'd finished dinner, though, Julie jumped to her feet. "Since you cooked, it's my job to clean up," she said as she stacked the dirty dishes together. "Why don't you and Lexi enjoy the sunset? This won't take long."

Was it his imagination, or did she seem nervous? "Lexi, let's help Julie carry everything inside."

His daughter was eager to assist, and soon they had the patio table cleared off. Because Julie was so determined to do the dishes, he went back outside with Lexi.

"Did you see that, Daddy?" Lexi said with excitement. "That was a firefly!"

"There's another one," he said pointing off to the right. As darkness fell, the winking lights from the fireflies became more noticeable. He had to laugh as Lexi ran around the yard, chasing the flashes of light and trying to capture them in the palms of her hands.

"It's so great to hear her laughing," Julie said as she came back outside.

"Yes, it is," he agreed. He leaned over and captured her hand to guide her into the chair beside him. "Hopefully, all that running around will tire her out," he added dryly.

Julie gently pulled her hand away and laced her fingers together in her lap. "You didn't have to come back to finish the townhouse, Derek," she said softly.

Did she really think that was the only reason he came back? "Yes, I did, because that was a good excuse to see you."

He heard her soft gasp of surprise and grew a bit concerned. Was it possible she didn't feel anything for him after all? The morning before, when he saw her crying in the courtroom, he thought for sure she cared about him. Maybe even had started to fall in love with him.

The way he'd fallen in love with her.

"Daddy, I caught one!" Lexi shouted.

"We have to talk," he said to Julie before getting up and crossing over to Lexi. It took some finagling, but he coaxed her into letting the lightning bug go so the little guy would be free to fly through the night with his friends.

"Time for bed, Lexi," he said. "Say goodnight to Julie."

"G'night, Julie," Lexi repeated, running over to give her a hug. "See you in the morning."

"Sounds good," Julie said. "Goodnight, Lexi."

He took his daughter inside and waited patiently for her to use the bathroom, brush her teeth, and then say her prayers, a new ritual for them.

Lexi closed her eyes and pressed her hands together. "God bless Mommy up in heaven, Grandma and Grandpa in St. Louis, Daddy and Julie here in Crystal Lake. Amen." Lexi opened her eyes. "That's everyone, right, Daddy?"

"That's right, baby-doll. I love you." He gathered her close for a tight hug and a kiss. "Sweet dreams."

"G'night, Daddy."

He headed back outside to Julie, trying to ignore the sudden attack of nerves. Thankfully, Julie was still sitting right where he'd left her, head tipped back as she gazed up at the stars.

"It's so beautiful up here," he said as he sat beside her. "Lexi was not happy when she discovered she couldn't see the stars in the city."

"I'm so glad everything worked out for you, Derek," Julie said softly.

"I accepted a new job," he said.

"Really? That's wonderful! I'm so glad Robert changed his mind."

Robert? Did she really think he'd planned on staying in St. Louis? "Julie, I accepted the dispatch job here at the Hope County Sheriff's Department. I start next Monday."

"You did? But why? You promised to let Robert and Gladys see Lexi on a regular basis. It's an eight-hour drive from here to their home in St. Louis!"

"I've promised them they'll get plenty of time with Lexi,"

he assured her. "But I happen to like it here in Crystal Lake. And so does Lexi."

"I...don't know what to say," she whispered. "I never expected you to come back here permanently."

He heard the doubt in her tone and decided enough was enough. He rose to his feet and pulled her up, too, so that he could wrap his arms around her. He gently brushed a strand of hair away from her face and cupped her cheek with the palm of his hand. "Julie, tell me that what I'm feeling isn't one-sided," he said in a pleading tone. "Tell me that you have some feelings for me, too."

"Oh, Derek." She wrapped her arms tightly around his waist. "I do, but are you sure about this? I feel like I should pinch myself to make sure I'm not dreaming."

"I've fallen in love with you, Nurse Julie," he whispered before claiming her sweet mouth with his. After a long moment, he lifted his head to catch his breath. As far as he was concerned, he could stand here under the stars and kiss Julie all night long. But he still needed to know that she felt the same way. "Lexi loves you, too. Is it too much to ask that you give us a chance?"

He could feel her draw an unsteady breath and tried not to fear the worst. "No, it's not too much to ask," she murmured. "But I was engaged once before, and, well, things didn't work out. So I have to be honest and tell you that this all feels like too much, too soon. You've always lived in the city, Derek. Living out here, it's nice, but the pace is slower. The winters can be long and brutal. I don't think you really understand what you're getting yourself into by moving up here."

"Enough with the weather report," he interjected with frustration. "Julie, I've spent a long time searching for someone to share my life with. As much as I cared about

Claire, I didn't love her the way I should have. I'm sorry if some jerk hurt you, but don't make me pay for his sins. Do you really think I'd risk my daughter's future if I wasn't sure about how much I love you?"

There was a long pause before she lifted herself up on her tiptoes and wrapped her arms around his neck. "I love you, too, Derek," she confessed before she kissed him again.

"Thank you, Lord," he said when he was able to breathe again. "You have no idea how hard I've been praying for this ever since you left me back in St. Louis."

"Me, too," she whispered. "Welcome home, Derek."

EPILOGUE

T*en months later...*

JULIE STOOD in the entryway of the small church, not the least bit nervous on her wedding day. The sun was shining, and there was a cool, May breeze coming off the lake. Lexi stood in front of her, wearing a miniature white gown and a ring of flowers in her hair.

"Ready, sweetie?" she asked when the organist began "The Wedding March."

"Yes, I'm ready." Lexi took her role of being the flower girl very seriously, holding on to her white basket of rose petals as if she were afraid she'd drop it. Julie smiled when she watched Lexi start down the aisle, dropping delicate red and pink petals along the way.

She glanced at Zack, who was discreetly pulling at the necktie of his tux. Her brother was escorting her down the aisle and standing in as Derek's best man. He'd come a long way over the past few months, and she was thrilled at the change in his demeanor. "Ready?" she asked.

"I'm ready if you are, Sis." Zack held out his arm, and Julie took his elbow, knowing their parents were there in spirit, gazing down from the heavens above.

She started down the aisle, not even noticing all the people who'd crowded into the small church. She only had eyes for Derek, who was breathtakingly handsome in his tux, standing straight and tall as he waited for her next to the pastor. As amazing as Derek looked in a tux, she thought he looked just as handsome in his new deputy uniform. He'd been promoted four months ago after two of the older officers had decided to step down into the dispatch positions, leaving the younger guys to the more grueling police work. She was so proud of everything Derek had accomplished in the past ten months. They'd put the side-by-side townhouse up for sale and had their eye on the perfect three-bedroom house on the lake. Plenty of room for more children, Derek had promised.

Looking at him now, she was humbled to see the love shining blatantly from his eyes.

And she knew the same expression was on her face as well.

"Take care of her," Zack said as he handed Julie over to Derek.

"I will," he promised.

She took Derek's hand and smiled up at him. She was the lucky one in this union, and as she exchanged vows with Derek, she knew that God had answered her prayers, too.

She was blessed to have finally found what she'd always wanted. A home and a family with Derek and Lexi.

C hapter One

"MERRY, I'm so glad you're here!" Janelle greeted her with a dramatic sigh as Merry entered the arena of the Hope County Hospital's Emergency Room. "I've been waiting forever for you to get here."

ER Charge Nurse Meredith Haines frowned at her nursing colleague. "What's the problem? I'm not late. I'm fifteen minutes early for my shift."

"I know, but look." Janelle jabbed her finger at the large whiteboard listing all the names of the current patients in the ER. "Leonard Marks is in room ten. He's been asking for you for the past five minutes. I've been trying really hard to keep him calm until you could get here."

Merry rolled her eyes. Janelle acted as if no one else was capable of taking care of Leonard. Sure, he was a mammoth of a man with a volatile psych history, but he'd been coming to the Hope County Hospital for his medical care long before she'd moved to Crystal Lake, a little over two years ago. Surely other nurses had taken care of him before?

"Okay, I'll go and see him," Merry said. "But I'm supposed to be in charge, so I'll need you to make out assignments while I'm talking to Leonard."

"Thanks," Janelle said with a sigh of relief, tucking a dark strand of hair behind her ear. "Don't worry, I'll take care of the assignments. Anything to help you out. I don't know how you manage to deal so well with Leonard. Honestly? The guy scares me to death."

Merry's smile was a bit forced as she walked toward Leonard's room. She wasn't about to explain that she'd had lots of practice dealing with angry, psychotic men because she'd learned from firsthand experience.

She hadn't known about her former boyfriend's psych diagnosis until he'd attacked her.

The thought of Blake finding her sent a shiver down her spine. After leaving Minneapolis, she'd covered her tracks carefully. If Blake hadn't found her in more than two years, she didn't think he'd suddenly show up now.

Unfortunately, she knew far more about the complex world of psychiatric healthcare than she'd ever wanted to know. At least, today, she could put her knowledge and experience to good use.

Moving very slowly, to avoid any abrupt gestures, Merry carefully slid open the glass door to room ten and eased inside.

_____

"HI LEONARD," she greeted him softly. "It's me, Merry."

"Merry! Where have you been?" Leonard demanded with the petulance of a small child, his gaze dark with reproach. "I've been waiting and waiting for you."

He was a full grown man of thirty-five, but his mind was that of a six-year-old. And often a bad tempered six-year-old, although she knew it wasn't his fault. Leonard had suffered a traumatic brain injury on top of his underlying schizophrenia, a combination that made him extremely difficult to manage.

Her stomach tightened when she didn't see any sign of Leonard's mother, Doreen. Had his mother dropped him off and then left? Normally, his mother stayed to help keep Leonard calm.

"I'm sorry, Leonard," she murmured, giving him a gentle

smile. "But I'm here now. So tell me, what made you decide
to come in to see us today?" Ironically, she'd learned
Leonard didn't like the term *hospital* so she avoided using
the reference if at all possible.

For a moment he looked truly bewildered. "I don't
know." He rose to his feet and began to pace. "I have that
feeling again. The one I don't like. The one that makes me
mad. I hear voices telling me to do bad things."

Merry swallowed a knot of apprehension. The last few
times Doreen brought Leonard to the ER, he'd complained
of similar issues. Leonard was under a court order to take
his psych meds, but his mother sometimes forgot. Merry
was afraid Doreen Marks might be in the beginning stages
of Alzheimer's disease. And if that was the case, Leonard
would soon be too much for his mother to handle, if he
wasn't already.

Without his medication, Leonard became lost in a sea of
confusion. And when Leonard got confused, he got angry.
And violent.

Leonard also had a medical history of poorly controlled
diabetes and high blood pressure, but she couldn't even
begin to examine him for his medical problems until she'd
calmed him down.

"It's okay, Leonard," she said soothingly, placing a hand
lightly on his arm. She was one of the few who could touch
him without causing him to fly off in a rage. He tolerated
women fairly well and, for once, her petite frame gave her
an advantage. But Leonard didn't like men, especially those
in uniform. When Leonard saw the police he went berserk,
probably because he knew from several bad experiences
that the arrival of the police meant he was taking a one-way
trip to the mental health complex in Madison. "I'm here
now. You know I'll take good care of you, right?"

"Right. Merry takes good care of me," he muttered as he pulled away from her and continued to pace. "Only Merry. No one else."

"All the nurses here take good care of you, Leonard. Not just me." She knew this odd dependence he had for her wasn't healthy. It wasn't as if she could possibly work every single day, all three shifts. "Don't worry, you're going to be fine."

The last time Leonard had come in, she'd succeeded in avoiding transferring him to the mental health facility. Once he'd taken meds to keep him calm, they'd evaluated his diabetes and his high blood pressure, making minor adjustments to his meds. By the end of the visit, he'd been able to go home with his mother, as docile as a bunny.

Maybe, just maybe, she'd be able to do that again. She wasn't sure who the doctor was on his team, but she needed to let him or her know that last time they'd started with a hefty dose of anti anxiety meds before getting him to take his usual dose of antipsychotic medication.

"Okay, Leonard, I want you to stay here. I'll be right back. I'm going to get your favorite treat. Do you remember what your favorite treat is?"

Leonard was easily six feet tall and weighed two hundred eighty pounds, but a tremulous smile bloomed on his broad, square face. "Chocolate pudding!"

"That's right, chocolate pudding," she agreed with a smile. Sugar free chocolate pudding in deference to his diabetes, but he didn't need to know that. "Now be good and I'll get your treat, okay?"

Leonard nodded and she sent up a silent prayer on Leonard's behalf as she slid from his room. The poor man suffered more than anyone should have to. Grinding up pills and hiding the powder in the chocolate pudding was normally not an acceptable way to give patients their meds but, thankfully, Leonard's court order allowed them to do just that. During previous visits she'd been worried that he'd notice the slightly bitter taste but, every time, he'd gobbled up the pudding without detecting anything amiss.

Merry found Dr. Katy Albrecht hovering behind the desk, waiting for her. "I've ordered the Ativan for Leonard," Dr. Katy said before Merry could say anything. "The pharmacist is entering it in the system now."

"Thanks." Relieved that they were on the same page, Merry went over to the galley to grab two chocolate puddings from the tiny fridge. Then she stopped at the automated medication dispensing machine. It didn't take long to pull out the medications, crush the pills, and mix the powder in the pudding.

Satisfied, she shoved the spoon into the pudding and headed back across the arena to Leonard's room.

"Merry?" The sound of her name in a familiar, deep voice stopped her in her tracks. She braced herself before turning around to face police officer Zack Crain, who looked far too attractive in his dark blue uniform. He was tall, with short, dark hair and brilliant green eyes. Ever since she'd met Zack at his sister's wedding, her pulse jumped erratically when she was around him.

"Zack?" Her voice squeaked and she tried to get a grip. She licked her lips and tried again. "Hi. What are you doing here? I thought you worked in Madison?"

"I'm picking up the belongings from one of our car crash victims as potential evidence," he said. "Have you seen my sister, Julie? I was hoping to talk to her while I'm here."

"I'm sorry, but Julie and Derek are out of town enjoying a vacation alone while Lexi visits with her grandparents. I'm dog-sitting for them while they're gone." Merry glanced nervously over her shoulder towards Leonard's room. "Listen, Zack, I have a patient who doesn't like police, so please don't be upset, but I need to ask you to leave."

"Leave?" His eyebrows shot up in surprise, but then he scowled. "Don't worry, I'll be out of here as soon as security brings me what I need."

Merry didn't have time to argue. "Just wait someplace else, out of sight, okay?"

She turned back towards Leonard's room, but it was too late. Through the glass door, Leonard was staring in horror at Zack. There was a loud crash as Leonard slammed the bed up against the wall in a fit of anger.

"No cops!" he bellowed, lumbering out of his room, waving his arms wildly. "No cops!"

"Leonard, calm down. It's okay. I have your treat!" Merry planted herself directly in front of him, in a pathetic attempt to distract him from Zack, who she hoped and prayed was quickly ducking out of sight. "Look at me, Leonard." She captured his gaze with her own. "It's Merry, remember? I've promised to take good care of you. And I have your favorite treat!"

For a moment she thought she'd reached him, but then she saw Zack move up next to her as if he intended to protect her.

"No cops!" Leonard screamed. With a horrible keening wail, he brutally shoved Merry aside, sending her flying backward into the unforgiving corner of the nurse's station as he made a mad dash for the front door.

Oomph! She hit the edge of the counter, hard enough to steal the breath from her body, her left shoulder taking the brunt of the blow. She thought someone shouted her name over the din, but then a horrible pain exploded in her head.

Poor Leonard she thought, before darkness and pain closed around her.

—————

ZACK STARED in horror when Merry flew into the side of the nurse's station. He heard her teeth snap together before she sailed backward, landing on the floor. Her head hit the linoleum with a sickening thud.

"Merry!" Zack was the first to reach her side, his heart thundering in his chest as he looked down at her pale, limp form. Most of the staff had gone to help bring the psychotic patient under control, and he knew he should have been helping, too, but he couldn't tear his gaze from Merry.

He forced himself to remember his basic medical training, but it wasn't easy. He gently lifted Merry's head to feel along the back of her scalp. His fingers came away wet. Stained red.

Blood. *She was bleeding.*

"Merry? Can you hear me?" He could barely hear himself, his heart was hammering so hard. "I'm here, and I won't leave you. Open your eyes, Merry. Can you talk to me?"

Nothing. She didn't move.

"I need some help over here," he called sharply, drawing a few stares from the group gathering around the patient who was still thrashing on the floor in spite of the pile of people trying to hold him down. He caught sight of a needle and syringe being plunged into the patient's thigh.

He couldn't suppress a flash of guilt, knowing that if he'd listened to Merry and left right away, this wouldn't have happened. But he hadn't understood the magnitude of danger. And when she faced the crazy man head on, he refused to leave her vulnerable and alone.

"Oh no, Merry!" A young female with deep red hair, wearing a long white lab coat, came to his aid. He figured she must be a doctor when she felt for Merry's pulse, and then pulled out a penlight to peer at her pupils.

"Can't we get her into a bed?" Zack asked. He didn't want to do anything that would hurt Merry, but he also didn't like seeing her stretched out on the floor.

Merry let out a soft moan and, despite her obvious pain, he was deeply relieved to know she was coming around.

"Try not to move." The female doctor's name tag identified her as Dr. Katy Albrecht. "We need to assess the extent of your injuries. Can someone get me a C-collar?" she called.

Given how hard her head had hit the floor, Zack assumed Merry had a concussion, but hopefully nothing worse. He assisted with lifting Merry's head just enough for Dr. Katy to get the cervical collar in place.

"Now we need a back board," Dr. Katy said, glancing up at the other staff members who huddled around Merry. "Which empty room can we use?"

"Room six is empty," a nurse by the name of Janelle said. "We can put Merry in there."

"Great, how's Leonard?" Dr. Katy asked in a distracted tone.

Zack assumed Leonard was the big man who'd gone crazy when he saw Zack's uniform. He glanced over the doctor's shoulder. The big man who'd been so crazy a few minutes ago was now being led back to his room by several of the staff the medications obviously working to calm him down. "He's fine from what I can tell," he told her.

"Here's the long board," Janelle said, hurrying over with a full-size plastic board with handles along the sides.

"We're going to roll Merry over on her side, and you're going to tuck the board underneath her, understand?" Dr. Katy addressed him as if he were one of her staff members.

He nodded, more than willing to help out if needed. "I have some basic first aid training, so I understand the concept of a log roll."

It took a few minutes to get Merry centered on the long board. Three other staff members helped him lift her up and carry her over to the empty room.

"My head hurts," Merry murmured, her face drawn with discomfort.

"Leonard knocked you down," Zack told her. "I'm sorry, Merry. I should have listened to you."

"Merry, I need you to stay still until we can clear you for fractures and a head injury," Dr. Katy chimed in. "Right now, we're going to get you entered into the computer system as a patient."

Merry's eyes widened. "A patient? But I have to work!"

"Not happening," Zack said, his voice harsher than he intended. He wasn't angry at Merry, but at himself. He forced himself to speak to her in a gentle tone. "You're going to do whatever the doctor tells you, okay?"

Dr. Katy nodded her approval and walked away, leaving the two of them alone.

Merry's amber gaze bored into his. "Sounds like you're not giving me much of a choice," she finally muttered.

"I know, and I'm sorry. I feel terrible about what happened, but we need to know how badly you're injured."

Zack resisted the urge to brush her reddish gold hair away from her cheek. He couldn't afford to get emotionally involved with Merry, no matter how much he liked her.

Even now, well past two years after he lost his wife and daughter within six months of each other, he fought to keep his emotions in a deep freeze. Why were they thawing now, for his sister's friend, Merry Haines? It wasn't fair, since he had no intention of getting emotionally involved ever again.

"Is Leonard okay?" Merry asked.

He admired her ability to worry about the big man who'd knocked her around like a rag doll. "He'll be fine. They managed to get him medicated and back into his room."

Merry closed her eyes for a moment, and the tiny pucker between her brows made him realize she was in pain. "Poor Leonard, it's not his fault."

As a police officer, Zack interacted with many people with psychiatric issues. But he had to admit that Leonard was one of the worst he'd ever seen. That moment when Merry had stepped in front of Leonard, trying to reason with him was burned into Zach's memory. She'd reminded him of a slender David facing down Goliath, except her sling-shot was a cup of chocolate pudding. Pudding that was now splattered all over the wall.

"You should have gotten out of the way," he said in a weary tone. "The man is more than twice your size."

"Normally, Leonard likes me," Merry whispered. "I thought I could get through to him. I didn't want him to get hurt."

He wasn't sure what to say since he knew very well it was his fault that Leonard lost control.

Zack scrubbed his hands over his face. He was due to return to Madison with the evidence he'd come to collect, but he couldn't bring himself to leave Merry like this. Especially since his sister, Julie, wasn't around to help. He remembered talking to Merry at Julie and Derek's wedding and, at the time, she'd mentioned she didn't have any family in the area.

Zack pulled up a chair next to Merry's bedside and sat down. Her eyes drifted closed, deep brackets of pain pulling at the corners of her mouth. Her face was incredibly pale, each freckle standing out starkly against her skin.

As much as he didn't want to get involved, he couldn't make himself leave. At least, not until he knew she was all right. She looked far too helpless lying there on the bed.

He closed his eyes and pressed the heels of his palms into his eyes. Once he would have prayed for Merry's recovery, but not anymore.

Unfortunately, God had stopped listening to him a long time ago.

Made in the USA
Columbia, SC
27 April 2024